RIDER

Satan's Fury MC-Memphis

L. WILDER

L. Wilder

Cover Design: Mayhem Cover Creations-
www.facebook.com/MayhemCoverCreations

Editor: Lisa Cullinan

Proofreader- Rose Holub @ReadbyRose

Proofreader: Honey Palomino

Teasers & Banners: Gel Ytayz at Tempting Illustrations

Personal Assistant: Natalie Weston PA

Catch up with the entire Satan's Fury MC Series today!
All books are FREE with Kindle Unlimited!

Summer Storm (Satan's Fury MC Novella)

His Promise (The Happy Endings Collection #3)

❋ Created with Vellum

Prologue

I was born and raised in Oakland, Tennessee, a small town where life revolved around farming and Friday night football. Hell, it didn't matter if you were rich or poor, young or old—everyone came out to the game on Friday night. It's what folks lived for. They'd pack the stands and cheer like there was no tomorrow, silently praying for a big win with each new play. It was those big wins that would help distract them from the crops that weren't coming in or the bills that were piling up. As the team's quarterback, I was one of the many players the crowd was shouting for, but I never heard their screams. As soon as I stepped out on that field, I was in the zone, not thinking about anything except getting that ball from point A to point B.

There was no greater feeling than standing there waiting for the snap. As soon as the ball was in my hands, I was ready. A rush of adrenaline would surge through me as I'd watch the opposing team make their advance. I could hear the sounds of helmets and shoulder pads slamming against each other as my offensive line held off the defense. I'd take a three-step drop, and once I was in the pocket, I'd quickly scan the field for my receiver. Knowing exactly where I was tossing the ball, it wouldn't be long before we were hanging a half dozen on the board. I was good, one of the best, and even when we didn't win the game, I always gave the fans something to talk about. My latest game was no different. I threw a pass that was risky. Some might even say it was too risky. My receiver was completely covered by the opposing team and it could've easily been picked off, but I saw a sliver of opportunity and took it. Just as I knew it would, the ball went straight into his hands, and he made the winning touchdown. The crowd went wild, and I left the field knowing I'd done what I'd set out to do.

I was feeling on top of the world when I'd left the locker room that night. Everything was going exactly as planned. After a few more great plays, I'd get that scholarship to play ball at UT and finally have my way out, because once I was gone, I'd never look back. I was headed out to my truck when my best friend, Bryce, shouted across the parking lot. "Yo, Caleb! You coming with us or what?"

He was standing next to Emmet's truck, another one of my good friends, and when I answered, "Yeah, I'm coming, but I'll have to drive. I gotta help my dad out in the morning," a look of disappointment crept over his face.

"Damn, man," Bryce complained. "After that game, you'd think your dad would give ya the day off or something!"

"Yeah, right. We both know that's never gonna happen." My father was a cotton farmer, and I'd been helping him bring in the crops since the time my feet could reach the pedals on the tractor. When I wasn't helping with the plowing, planting, or picking, I was doing what I could to help prepare to plow, plant, or pick. I'd work on the farm equipment, haul trailers back and forth from the gin, and whatever else he needed me to do. While my dad loved everything about farming, it just wasn't my thing, and I was always relieved when football season rolled around. It was the only time he didn't complain about me not being out in the fields.

I could hear the others calling out to Bryce, telling him to hurry, so I said, "You guys go ahead. I'll see you over at Landon's in a few minutes."

"You know, Janey Thompson was asking about ya earlier."

"Yeah?"

"Sure was." A smile crossed his face as he opened the door to Emmet's truck. "She's gonna be there tonight. If you play your cards right, you might just get you some of that."

"I can have Janey Thompson any day of the week," I boasted, then murmured under my breath, "and so can every other football player in town."

"Guess we'll see about that tonight!"

Before I could respond, he'd climbed into the truck with the rest of the gang and closed the door. Clearly eager to get to the party, Emmet slammed his foot on the accelerator, hurling loose gravel from his rear tires. Unimpressed by his redneck display, I went over to my truck and tossed my stuff in the backend, then got inside and cranked the engine. By the time I started to pull out of the parking lot, most everyone had already gone. The only ones left were the coach and the cleaning crew, or so I thought.

I was just about to pull out onto the main road when I

noticed Darcy Harrington's beat-up pickup truck parked across the street. The hood was up with the taillights flashing, so I assumed it had broken down on her. As I sat there staring at her flashing lights, a battle ensued between my ears. I'd always been the kind of guy who'd lend a hand whenever someone needed it, especially when it came to women, but Darcy wasn't like most women.

When we were kids, Darcy and I were actually pretty good friends. We'd hang out on the school playground during recess, eat lunch together, and even run around at football games, but things were simpler then. There was no judging one another by the clothes we wore or the houses we lived in, but as we grew older that changed. Like a slow turn of the wind, we started talking less and less, and it wasn't long before we didn't say a word to one another, even in the hallway. That didn't mean I stopped noticing her. Hell, there wasn't a soul around who didn't pay attention when Darcy Harrington walked by. The tomboy with pigtails and freckles sprinkled across the bridge of her nose had turned into a beautiful girl with long auburn hair and curves that would give a *Playboy* model a run for her money.

Darcy's looks weren't the only thing that changed over the years. Where she was once sweet and funny, she'd become cold and detached—never letting anyone get too close. Her strong persona made her come off as unapproachable, so everyone kept their distance, fearing if they crossed her there'd be hell to pay. It was no wonder why Darcy acted the way she did. Her family was rough. They were the kind of folks you didn't want to cross in a dark alley—mean and mouthy, and didn't think twice about breaking the law. I didn't know their whole story, but from

what I'd heard, you didn't mess with the Harringtons—
especially Darcy.

I sat there a few more minutes, listening to my engine
idle and the monotonous tick of my blinker as I questioned my next move: I could head on over to the party,
toss back a few beers, and spend some *quality time* with
Janey Thompson, or risk getting my balls handed to me by
the very girl who'd starred in every one of my fucking wet
dreams since middle school. Before I even realized what I
was doing, I'd pulled out onto the road and was headed in
Darcy's direction. When I parked behind her truck, she
peeked her head around the hood and watched with a
blank expression as I got out and started towards her. "Is
everything okay?"

"Take a look around, Sport." Her words dripped with
sarcasm as she barked, "I'm out here alone in the dark,
parked on the side of the road with my flashers on, and my
hood up. I'd say those are pretty good signs that things are
not okay."

Ignoring her sour tone, I continued towards the front
of the truck. When I reached her, I asked, "You got any
idea what's wrong with it?"

"The battery cable's loose," she grumbled.

Even in the dark, I could see that Darcy looked
fucking incredible. She was wearing a pair of tight-fitting
jeans with a low-cut tank top, showing just a hint of cleavage, and the silver bangles around her wrist jingled when
she reached into her back pocket for her cigarettes. After
lighting one up, she announced, "My numb-nut brother
snatched my tools, and now I don't have a way to fix the
stupid thing."

I leaned in to take a closer look, and even though I

already knew the answer, I asked, "Would a crescent wrench do the trick?"

"Yeah, it would." A hopeful expression crossed her face. "Do you have one?"

"Hold on, let me see." I rushed back over to the truck and grabbed my tools. Once I found the wrench, I brought it over to her. "Got it."

"Well, how about that." After tossing her cigarette to the ground, she took the wrench from my hand, then handed me a flashlight. "You mind holding this?"

"Sure." I pointed the light at the battery. "This good?"

"Perfect."

She leaned forward with her phenomenal ass perched in the air, and I had to fight the urge to readjust myself as I stood there watching her reconnect the cables. Damn, I'd never seen anything so fucking hot in my entire life, and it took all I had not to reach out and grab her into my arms. Once she'd adjusted the bolt, she walked over to the driver's side of the truck and got inside. When she turned the ignition and pressed the gas several times, the truck sputtered a bit, then finally roared to life. Darcy turned to me with a smile. "Looks like Sport saves the day again."

"Again?"

"Yeah...that pass you threw to win the game. It was really something."

She walked back to the front of her truck and closed the hood. As she handed me my wrench, I asked, "You saw that, huh?"

"I did." She gave me a slight smirk. "You made the good folks of Oakland very proud tonight. I'm sure they'll be talking about it for weeks."

"I got lucky."

"We both know that play took a lot more than just

luck. Besides, I don't put much value in luck. Either you have it or you don't. Simple as that." She walked by me and got inside her truck. "Thanks for giving me a hand tonight. I appreciate it."

"Anytime." It was the most we'd spoken in the last couple of years, and I wasn't ready for her to go. Trying to play it cool, I told her, "Landon Creasey's having a party out at his place."

"Doesn't he have a party every Friday night?" she scoffed.

"He does." I knew it was a reach, but I had to try. "You should stop by."

"Thanks for the invite, Sport, but I don't think so. High school parties and I just don't mix." She closed her door and leaned her head out the window. "So, you working with your dad tomorrow or whatever?"

Surprised she knew anything about me, my brows furrowed. "Yeah, why?"

"What time will you get done?"

"Some time after dark...maybe eight."

She studied me for a moment, then said, "You know the old racetrack down by Eastman's grocery?"

"Yeah?"

"Meet me there tomorrow night at nine."

I nodded and replied, "I'll be there."

"Good." A soft smile crossed her face, and the whole world stopped spinning. Damn, I'd always thought that Darcy was beautiful, but when she smiled, she was absolutely stunning. I couldn't take my eyes off her as she shifted the truck into drive. Before pulling away, she waved and said, "See ya tomorrow night."

She was already out of earshot when I shouted, "Looking forward to it!"

I was in a complete daze while I stood there and watched her taillights fade into the night. I couldn't believe Darcy Harrington had just asked me on a date, or at least, I thought it was a date. At that moment, I didn't really care; it was enough to put a smile on my face. I headed back to my truck, and when I started the engine, I saw that it was almost midnight. Knowing I had to get up early in the morning, I decided to skip the party and head home. When I got to the house, I wasn't surprised to find that the lights were out and everyone had already gone to bed. I went into the kitchen and grabbed a quick bite to eat, then started up to my room. Just as I topped the stairs, my mother called out to me. "Caleb?"

I turned back and found her standing in her doorway with a concerned expression. "Yeah?"

"You're home early. Is everything okay?"

"Yeah, everything's good."

"Okay, good." She smiled as she said, "You played a great game tonight."

"We did all right."

"You did more than all right, Caleb." When I didn't respond, she asked, "You going to set your alarm, or do you want me to wake you?"

"I've got it, Mom," I assured her. "Go back to bed."

"Okay. Good night."

"Night."

I went on to my room and crawled into bed. As I lay there, a smile crept over my face when my mind drifted back to Darcy. Our brief encounter had made quite an impression on me, and I found myself looking forward to the following night when I'd get the chance to know her even better. I was feeling pretty damn positive about things. My chances to play at UT were looking good, and I had a date with none other than Darcy Harrington. As I drifted off to sleep, I couldn't imagine things being any better. Sadly, the following morning, my life took a drastic turn.

With one fleeting moment—one stupid, careless mistake, I lost everything. My chance with Darcy. My football scholarship at UT. My friends. My family. Hell, I'd lost my entire life as I knew it, and to make matters worse, I'd done it all to myself.

Rider

❧

I was busy working in the garage when I heard Blaze ask, "Everything all right there?"

I glanced over my shoulder and found him pacing back and forth in his office as he held his cellphone up to his ear. I could tell by the tone in his voice and the expression on his face that he was talking to his ol' lady, Kenadee. The poor guy had been worried sick about her for days, calling her job every few hours to make sure she was okay, even though he knew one of the prospects was there at the hospital watching over her. I could hear the relief in his voice when he continued, "Good. So, no sign of the Disciples?"

He paused, giving Kenadee a chance to respond, then told her, "I'm aware I asked you that two hours ago, and I got news for you...I'm gonna ask you again and again until I'm sure those motherfuckers are going to leave you the fuck alone."

Kenadee is a triage nurse at Regional Hospital. If she was working anywhere else, it might not have been so bad, but being an emergency room nurse at one of the biggest hospitals in the city of Memphis was tough. Night after night, she dealt with gunshot wounds, stabbings, overdoses, and God knows what else, but Kenadee loved her job. Blaze, on the other hand, didn't feel the same way. He believed that it was too dangerous for her to work there, and the other night we all realized just how right he was. Kenadee was working the graveyard shift when a kid came in with multiple gunshot wounds and was barely hanging on. They did everything they could to save him, but he was simply too far gone. His father immediately lost it, shouting and tossing shit everywhere. When the cops came to escort him out, he threatened Kenadee, warning her that he was going to make her pay for letting his boy die.

It wasn't the first time she'd gotten threats, but this time it was different. This time, it was Keshawn Lewis. He was known by the name "Slayer" and was the leader of the Inner Disciples' gang. When he threatened Kenadee's life, Blaze was understandably troubled that he'd make good on his promise. Because of that concern, Blaze brought Kenadee and his son, Kevin, to stay at the clubhouse. He knew we'd do everything in our power to ensure her safety.

Before he ended the call, he told her, "Love you, too, babe. I'll be there at six when you get off."

Blaze shoved his phone in his back pocket, then turned his attention back to the stack of paperwork on his desk. He was in charge of the garage and took his job very seriously, always making sure everything ran smoothly. After several minutes, he stepped out into the main garage and shouted, "Hey, Murph? How much longer on the Chief?"

"I'll be done on my end in an hour or so," he answered from the back of the garage. "I've got everything broken down. Just need to finish prepping for paint."

"Good. Maybe we can have it all wrapped up by the end of the week."

"You know, it'd go a lot faster if we were able to get the painting done here," Murphy complained.

"I know. I'm working on it. Hope to know something this afternoon."

"What happens this afternoon?"

"Riggs is doing a background check on that girl T-Bone suggested hiring. If everything checks out, I'm going over to see if she's interested in taking the position."

"We could really use the help around here," Murphy complained. "Do what you gotta do to get her ass over here."

"You know I will." Blaze assured him. "Just let me know when you're done, and I'll get everything across town."

"You taking the Honda, too?"

"I would, but Rider just started on it two days ago. No way he's done with her yet."

"Actually, she's ready when you are," I told him.

"What?" Blaze looked over at me, surprised. "You're done?"

"Yep." I nodded. "Finished everything up last night."

"Damn, brother. You didn't have to go and do that."

"I know. I just wanted to do what I could to help out."

When I started prospecting for the club, I quickly realized I'd been given a second chance. It wasn't something I thought I deserved, not after all I'd done, but Gus, the president of Satan's Fury, didn't agree. He saw something in me that no one else did. Without even asking anything in return, he and the brothers helped me turn my life around. That in itself was enough to make me forever grateful, so I always tried to do more than what was expected. It was the only way I knew how to show my appreciation. I motioned my hand over to the Ford pickup I'd been working. "A few more minutes, I'll have Mr. Pruitt's water pump sorted."

"You trying to make the rest of us look bad or something?" T-Bone taunted.

Before I could answer, Gunner looked over to him and snickered. "Not like you make that too hard for him."

"He's right," Blaze added. "Hell, we've been waiting on you to finish that fucking gas tank for two days."

"Hold up. I can't help it that the damn thing had a fucking leak," T-Bone complained. "With all this damn humidity, it took forever for the fucking epoxy to cure."

Gunner chuckled as he mumbled, "Excuses. Excuses."

T-Bone was about to argue further when Blaze cut him off. "Look, we don't have time to be fucking around here, guys. We have a lot of shit to finish up, and Gus wants us over at the clubhouse at seven for church."

"You got any idea why?" I asked. "Is something up?"

"Got no idea. Guess we'll all find out together."

I nodded, then got back to work installing the water pump on Pruitt's truck. After I finished, I went over and helped Tank finish with the gas tank and rear fender. By the time we had everything sandblasted and ready for paint, it was almost five and time to close up shop. We had just enough time to grab a hot shower and a bite to eat before we had to meet up with Gus for church. Once we'd locked up the garage, I followed T-Bone and Gunner back to the clubhouse, while Blaze and Murphy took the bike parts over to the paint shop and picked up Kenadee from the hospital. As soon as I got back to the clubhouse, I went to my room and took a shower. Once I threw on some fresh clothes, I headed down the hall to the kitchen to find something to eat. Several of the hang-arounds were busy making lasagna with all the fixings. Gunner, and Shadow, the club's enforcer, were already sitting at the table eating with our VP, Moose, and his ol' lady, Louise. I was about to make myself a plate when Jasmine, one of the hang-arounds, came up to me. "Hey there, good lookin'. You want me to make you a plate?"

I wasn't one to let others do for me what I could do myself, so I shook my head. "No. I'll get it, but thanks."

"You sure? I don't mind."

"I'm sure."

I made my way over to the stove, and after I fixed myself a plate of lasagna and garlic bread, I went over and sat down at the table next to Gunner. Just as I was about to start eating, he looked over to me and said, "You should've told me you were going back to the garage to work last night. I would've given you a hand."

"I know. That's why I didn't mention it." Gunner was a good guy—one of the best. He'd have to be, otherwise Gus would've raised all kinds of hell when he found out about Gunner and his daughter, August. After she showed up at the clubhouse looking for help with finding her daughter, Harper, Gus ordered Gunner to watch after her and keep her safe. Gunner did what he could to fight the pull he felt towards her, but from early on, he knew she was the one for him. Once Harper was returned and the issues with August's ex were resolved, Gunner and August started planning their future together. After all they'd been through, I knew he needed to be spending time with them, not helping me at the garage. "With the move and all, I'm sure August and Harper want you home with them."

"Yeah, but they'd understand if you needed me," he pushed.

"Maybe so, but it wasn't a big deal." Before I took a bite of my lasagna, I added, "Besides, I managed fine on my own."

"You know, you're gonna have to stop doing that at some point."

"Doing what?"

"That thing where you keep trying to prove yourself." He smacked my shoulder. "You've already done that, brother. Otherwise, you wouldn't be sportin' that patch."

"Not about that," I started. "I'm just trying to do my part."

"We both know it's more than that."

He was right. It was so much more than that, but I found it doubtful that he'd understand. Hell, there were times when I didn't understand the shit that was going through my head, so there was no sense talking about it. Thankfully, Blaze came over and sat down next to us, drawing Gunner's attention away from me and over to him. "Kenadee make it okay today?"

"Yeah. No sign of any trouble."

"Good. Maybe this thing with the Disciples will just blow over, and Kenadee can put this shit behind her."

"Damn, I hope so, but I got a feeling that ain't gonna happen." Before Blaze took a bite of lasagna, he said, "But on a good note, I think we've got ourselves a new painter for the garage."

"That chick from Thompson's garage?" Gunner questioned.

"Yeah. Everything checked out on the background check Riggs did on her. Grew up in Oakland, and since she left there, she keeps pretty much to herself. No boyfriend or husband to speak of, just a couple of brothers who give her shit from time to time, so I offered her the job." Blaze was clearly pleased as he said, "She's agreed to come down to the shop tomorrow and look things over, which is great cause this chick's got real talent. Since she started working with Thompson, his business has almost doubled. If she takes us up on our offer, Thompson's gonna be pissed."

I didn't have to ask who they were talking about. I already knew it was Darcy Harrington. I could still remember the day T-Bone suggested that the club offer her the job; I shouldn't have been surprised that her name came up though. Darcy was extremely talented. In fact, she was one of the best custom painters around, but it didn't change the fact that I hoped they wouldn't hire her. It wasn't her fault that I felt the way I did. She was simply a part of my past, and any time I thought about her, the memories of that morning and the months thereafter would come flooding back. I'd spent the last couple of years trying to forget them, but I was slowly learning that I could no more avoid them than the beating of my own heart.

Blaze looked over to me as he asked, "You grew up in Oakland, right?"

"Yeah, I did."

"So, did you know her?"

"I did," I admitted. "It was a small town. We all knew each other, but that was a long time ago." Without even realizing it, I'd started rubbing my right arm, trying to ease the dull ache that had started to throb deep within the muscles and old scar tissue. Concerned, Gunner leaned towards me and asked, "You all right, brother?"

"Yeah," I lied. "My arm's just acting up."

"You should see if Doc can give you something for it," Blaze suggested.

Unfortunately, there was no drug and no amount of alcohol on this earth that could ease the pain I was feeling. I'd already tried. Damn near killed myself searching for something to numb the ache. It wasn't until I started prospecting for Fury that I discovered something that'd give me any relief and that was riding my Harley. My bike gave me an even greater rush than I'd felt when I was playing ball. I needed that distraction right now, but it would have to wait. We had church in a few minutes, so I released the hold on my arm and replied, "No need for that. I'll be fine."

"You sure?"

"Absolutely."

When I turned my attention back to my food, Gunner did the same, and by the time we were all done, it was time for church. I followed Gunner and Blaze into the conference room, and we joined the others at the table. As soon as we were all seated, Gus turned to us and said, "You all know, the leader of the Inner Disciples made a threat against Kenadee a couple of weeks ago. Riggs has been doing what he can to monitor the situation, watching the security feed at all their hangouts, and we both have our concerns about Lewis's current behavior."

"Why? What the fuck is he doing?" Blaze asked.

"Lewis doesn't run his crew like most of the gangs around here. He's been a loose cannon, driven by the ownership of his turf and vengeance, but for the most part, he's stayed clean. Recently, he's been cracked out on coke, involved in shootouts with neighboring gangs, and the other night, a few of his boys robbed a downtown pawnshop. They got a pretty damn good take on AR15s and Glocks. If I didn't know better, I'd say they were making preparations."

Murphy leaned forward and asked, "Preparations for what?"

"No way to know for sure. Just be on high alert," Gus warned. "If this guy tries to make good on his threats, I want you ready."

"Understood," we all replied.

"Good. Church is dismissed."

We all stood and started to disperse. Like most nights, some of the brothers went to the bar to toss back a few beers, while others went home to their ol' ladies. I didn't have a woman and wasn't in the mood for drinking, so I started towards the parking lot. I was just about to walk out the back door when I overheard Blaze talking to Gus. I could hear the mix of relief and excitement in his voice as Blaze told him, "We'll have to see how it goes. She's coming first thing tomorrow morning to check it out and see if she's interested in working with us."

"You sure it's a good idea to bring a woman into the garage?"

"This Darcy chick has real talent, Gus, and Thompson hasn't had any problems with her working at his place."

Gus's tone grew harsh as he replied, "Yeah, well... Thompson isn't using his garage as a front for his club."

Blaze ran his hand over his beard. "I don't know what to tell you, Prez. There's a lot I don't know about this chick, but I've got a good feeling about her."

"We'll have Riggs look into her and make sure she's not someone we'll need to be concerned about."

Damn. From the sounds of it, Blaze had his mind set on hiring Darcy Harrington. The thought didn't set well with me as I headed out to the parking lot. I got on my bike, turned the ignition, and seconds later, I was pulling out of the gate. As soon as I hit the open road, I turned back the throttle and disappeared into the night. It's hard to explain how alive I felt at that moment, like I was completely in tune with the world around me. When I was on my bike, I could see things more clearly, smell every scent, feel the wind against my skin, and hear the sounds of the city echoing around me. As I leaned my bike into a winding turn, it was just me and the road ahead. I wasn't thinking about Darcy Harrington or my past, and in no time, the tension I'd been carrying all night started to fade. I rode for several hours, and when exhaustion started to set in, I went back to the clubhouse to crash for the night. By the time I walked into my room, I could barely keep my eyes open. I thought for sure I'd go straight to sleep, but unfortunately, that didn't happen. Instead, I spent the entire night tossing and turning as I thought about coming face to face with Darcy Harrington again. I had a feeling that it wouldn't be a happy reunion for either of us.

Darcy

I'd been working overtime for days and was exhausted, so I'd gone to bed early in hopes of actually getting a decent night's rest. I'd been sleeping for several hours when I heard a jangling noise coming from across the room. I didn't have to get up and look to know that it was Scout, my sweet, but pain-in-the-ass cat, who was making all the racket. Whenever she got bored, she'd start fiddling with Lenny's cage. She loved pestering that silly rabbit, but no more than he loved pestering her. I tried ignoring them, but their horsing around caused the entire cage to rattle and it just kept getting louder and louder. I reached for a pillow and placed it over my head, hoping to muffle the irritating sound. Unfortunately, that didn't work either. Frustrated, I took the pillow and tossed it across the room as I fussed, "Come on, guys! I'm trying to sleep over here!"

The noise quickly stopped, and I was relieved that the room fell silent. I curled back into my pillow and closed my eyes. I could feel myself sinking into the mattress and was just starting to doze back off when Scout started walking up my leg. She stopped after she reached my hip, then started pawing at the comforter while trying to make herself a spot to lay down. I lifted my head and glared at her. "Really?"

Ignoring me, she continued about her business. I gave her a little nudge, forcing her off of me, and tried once more to go back to sleep. As I lay there with my eyes closed for several minutes, I quickly realized that it was a lost cause. Wide awake and frustrated, I tossed back the covers and started towards my tiny kitchen. My house trailer wasn't anything fancy. In fact, it was pretty run down with a hodgepodge of furniture I'd collected from yard sales and Goodwill, but it was mine. Even though it wasn't much, I'd worked hard to piece it together, and I was proud of it. As I started making my coffee, I noticed the sunlight began to trickle through the cheap mini-blinds and decided that getting up was probably for the best. It wouldn't be long before I'd have to head over to meet with Blaze at the Satan's Fury garage. I was still trying to wrap my head around the fact that he'd offered me a chance to come work for them. I'd heard the rumors about Satan's Fury. I knew they weren't your regular MC. These men were dangerous, and it was hard to believe that such a powerful group of men had asked me, *a woman*, into their den of wolves.

I wanted to make sure I was ready in plenty of time, so I finished off my coffee then headed into the bathroom for a quick shower. Scout sat on the end of the bed, watching as I got dressed and pulled my hair back into a ponytail. Once I was done, I walked over and ran my hand down her head and back. "Hold down the fort. I'll be back when I can."

After I checked myself in the mirror once last time, I grabbed my keys and wallet, then headed outside to my motorcycle. My 2015 Kawasaki H2R was one of my most prized possessions. While my so-called crotch-rocket wasn't for everyone, I loved everything about it, especially the way she could hug a turn at eighty miles an hour. I slipped on my helmet, and seconds later I was on my way into town. It was a thirty-minute drive, but I didn't mind. It gave me a chance to clear my head and prepare myself for the day ahead. I'd hoped that it would do the same for me today, but as I got closer to the city, I could feel my nerves starting to set in. I wasn't exactly sure what had me so worked up. It wasn't like I'd never been around men like those in Satan's Fury. Hell, I'd grown up with criminals and neighborhood thugs, so I knew how to handle myself. As I pulled up into their garage's parking lot, I tried to convince myself that I had nothing to be nervous about, but it didn't work. My stomach was in knots as I got off my bike, and I silently cursed myself for being such a damn girl as I removed my helmet.

I inhaled a deep breath and was doing my best to pull my shit together when I heard someone call out to me. "Hey, Darcy! Come around to the back."

"Okay. Be right there."

The time had officially come. I had to put on my big girl panties and show these badass bikers that they would be lucky to have me on their time. When I got to the back door, Blaze was standing there waiting for me. "Morning."

"Morning."

"I appreciate you coming by like this." He motioned me forward. "Come on in, and I'll show you around."

As I followed him inside, I felt the stares of the club members burning against my flesh. I took a quick glance around, trying to see who it was that made me feel so uneasy, but all the guys seemed to be busy working—not looking at me. I shook it off, thinking it was just my imagination playing tricks on me and turned my focus back to Blaze. "Looks like you guys are doing really well here."

"We do all right." There was no missing the pride in his voice as he spoke. "My brothers and I have been working hard to expand our restoration abilities, so we can do everything in-house. That's why we've asked you here. We don't want to keep sending our parts out when we could do it right here in the garage."

"Do you have the space and equipment that you'll need?"

"We're working on it." He led me over to a door, and when he opened it, I could see that they'd added a small room to the rear corner of the building. "To pass inspection, you're gonna need a ventilation system that filters out the flammable contaminants."

"It's in the works." He pointed to the ceiling as he said, "We're putting an independent exhaust system in place to discharge outside of the building. It'll run at all times during and after spraying."

"Sounds good." I stepped inside the room and had to admit, I was impressed. They had put a lot of work into building just the right setup, and the equipment they'd purchased was top of the line. "Looks like you have everything in order."

"Yeah, except we're missing one crucial element." He cocked his eyebrow as he looked over to me and said, "We need ourselves a painter, and not just any painter. We need the best, and that's where you come into play."

I took another look around the room as I mulled things over. I had a good thing going at Thompson's garage, but Blaze was offering me twice the pay and a chance at commissions for any business I brought into the shop. With money like that, I could move out of my janky trailer and find a place in the city. It was a deal I couldn't pass up, but I had one more question that needed to be answered before I could accept the position. I turned to Blaze and studied him for a moment before asking, "You sure your boys can handle having a woman work in their garage?"

"It might take some getting used to, but they'll manage." His eyes quickly skirted over me as he scoffed. "Something tells me that you won't give them much choice in the matter."

"You're right about that." I turned and started for the door. "I have a couple of projects at Thompson's that I'll need to finish up before I can start."

As he followed me back into the garage, he asked, "That mean you're in?"

"Yeah, I'm in."

Just as the words left my mouth, I saw him, and my stomach dropped to my knees. I couldn't move. I just stood there frozen, staring at him like a deer in headlights as I tried to make sense of who I was seeing. Caleb Hughes, the boy who drove all the girls wild with his devilish good looks and charming smile had traded in his football pads for a Satan's Fury cut. His dark hair was longer now, shaggier, and down over his brow, making it difficult to see his eyes. But I remembered how dark and soulful they were. With just one look, he could make you feel like he knew all your deepest secrets. There was a time when I thought of him as a friend, a good friend, but eventually that friendship dwindled away—probably because I stopped talking to him. Things at home were difficult, and even though I knew Caleb would've been there for me, I was too embarrassed to let him know what was going on. I could remember that night like it was yesterday. My truck had broken down, and he'd stopped to help me. It had been years since we'd actually spoken to each other, and while it was a short encounter, it felt good to reconnect with him. As I looked at him now, he was nothing like the young handsome boy who'd come to my rescue. Where he used to be tall and lean, he was now all man—gruff and all kinds of sexy with bulging muscles and tattoos. I was still marveling at his transformation when I heard Blaze say, "Good deal. I'll let the guys know."

I nodded, then we continued towards the back door. Just before I walked out, I turned to Blaze and said, "I should be able to start at the beginning of next week."

"Great. We should have the ventilation system installed by then."

"Sounds good. I'll see you then."

Feeling a mix of excitement and apprehension over my new job, I walked out of the garage and headed over to my bike. Moments later, I was on my way to work. Like I'd mentioned to Blaze, I had several projects that I intended to finish, and I had to talk to Mr. Thompson. I wasn't looking forward to telling him that I'd accepted Blaze's offer. He'd always been decent to me, treating me more like a father figure than a boss, and even though it would mean losing me to the competition, he didn't discourage me from going to see their garage. Mr. Thompson worked with their club for years, and even with their ominous reputation, he thought a lot of them. When I got to the shop, he was in his office working on invoices, but quickly stopped as soon as he spotted me standing in front of his desk. It was like he knew what was coming as soon as he looked at up at me, and with a grimace, he asked, "Well?"

"They have a pretty good setup over there."

"Yeah, I told you they would." He took off his glasses as he studied me for a moment. "You accepted his offer, didn't you?"

"It's a lot of money." I shrugged as I said, "I could finally get a place in the city."

"I know. I get it." He stood up, walked over to me, and as he placed his hands on my shoulders, he said, "You've done good, Darcy. Real good. I can't blame you for wanting to take that job. It's a lot of money, and you deserve every damn penny of it. I just wish I had the means to pay you like that."

"I really appreciate everything you've done for me, and I'm gonna stay until I finish up my current projects. Also, Samuel is really getting the hang of things since I've been working with him. I don't think he'll have a problem taking over."

"Sam's a good kid, but he'll never have talent like yours."

I tried to comfort him by saying, "I don't know. He might surprise you."

"We'll see." He gave me a quick hug. "You best get to work. I promised Rice we'd have his Mustang back to him by tomorrow afternoon."

"I'm on it."

I left his office and dove straight into what I'd been working on. Everyone was long gone by the time I'd finished the trim work on Rice's Mustang, so I was left to close things down for the night. I hit all the lights, and once I'd locked up everything, I went out to my bike and headed home. When I pulled up to the trailer park, I wasn't surprised to see that Mrs. Alice and Mrs. Frances were sitting out on their front porch. The sweet, little old ladies were out there every night, gossiping about everything that went on in our small community, and I had no doubt that I was often the topic of their conversations and really couldn't blame them. I was the youngest one living in the Shady Pines Trailer Park, followed by Mr. Sanders, who had to be at least seventy years old. I was single, living alone, and rode a motorcycle, which was enough to make anyone curious, especially little old ladies with a lot of free time on their hands.

After I took off my helmet, I waved at Mrs. Alice and Mrs. Frances. "Hey, ladies. You two having a nice night?"

"We certainly are," Mrs. Frances answered. "We just had us a bowl of peach cobbler, and it was simply divine. Would you like some?"

As much as I hated to admit it, I kind of liked that Mrs. Alice and Mrs. Frances looked out for me like they did. They were always making extra casseroles for me and even checked in on me whenever I wasn't feeling good. It was the first time in my life that I had anyone who actually wanted to take care of me, and it meant a great deal. While I loved their cooking and had no doubt that the cobbler would taste amazing, I really wasn't in the mood for it. I ran my hand over my stomach and smiled as I told her, "I wish I could, Mrs. Frances, but I've gotta watch my figure and all that."

"Oh, you silly child. You look wonderful." She shook her head as she mumbled, "What I wouldn't give to be your age again with a figure like that. I'd give the men around here a run for their money."

"Something tells me you turn plenty of heads around here." She was wearing one of her duster gowns with a flower pattern and sock slippers, and her freshly curled gray hair had a purple hue to it, letting me know that she'd just paid a visit to the salon. "You're looking pretty hot with that new do of yours."

She patted the back of her hair with the palm of her hand as she replied, "I just had it done."

"I can tell. It looks great." I looked over to Mrs. Alice and smiled as I asked, "Is that a new gown, Mrs. Alice?"

"It sure is," she answered proudly. "Linda came by this afternoon and brought it to me. What do you think?"

Linda was her daughter, and even though she'd never say it, we all knew it bothered Alice that Linda didn't come by to see her more often. "I think it looks amazing on ya. She picked out the perfect color."

"You are just the sweetest child." My heart warmed when I saw the proud smile on her face. She motioned inside her trailer as she said, "There's plenty of cobbler if you change your mind."

"I appreciate it." As I started up my steps, I waved at them both and said, "You two try and behave yourselves."

"We'll try!"

The second I unlocked my door and stepped inside, Scout came rushing over to me, meowing and rubbing her body against my legs. It was her way of telling me she was hungry. "Okay, okay. Give me a second."

I poured some cat food into her bowl, then went over and fed Lenny. As soon as they were both tended to, I took a hot shower. Once I'd put on a clean t-shirt, I headed back into the kitchen and warmed up a couple of slices of leftover pizza, then carried it into the bedroom. I was exhausted. I just wanted to eat and go to sleep, so I didn't even bother turning on the TV. After taking a few bites of pizza, I'd had enough and placed the plate on the table next to my bed. I turned off the light and scooted down into the covers, being careful not to disturb Scout as she slept at the foot of my bed. I closed my eyes, and it wasn't long before my mind drifted to Caleb. A smile crossed my face when I thought back to the days we'd see who could swing higher on the school's swing set. It'd felt so freeing with the wind blowing in my hair, the sun shining down on my face, and him by my side that I wasn't thinking about how bad things were at home. It was just Caleb and me, and nothing else mattered. Sadly, that all changed the day my older brother brought me back to reality.

I'd just walked in from school. Dad was passed out on the sofa, and my older brothers, Danny and Eddie, were standing in the kitchen, staring into our empty refrigerator. As usual, the camper was a mess. There were dirty dishes piled up in the sink and empty beer cans littered the countertops and floors. I must've made a face that Eddie didn't like because he barked, "What's with you?"

"Nothing," I lied.

"Don't give me that shit." He slammed the refrigerator door and took a step towards me. "I know that look. I've seen it plenty of times before."

I was only eleven at the time and had no idea what he was talking about. "What look?"

"The look that says you think you're too good to be here, living in this shithole with us," he spat. "Thing is, you never had a fucking problem with it before."

"I don't have a problem with anything."

It was a complete and total lie. I hated that we were so poor that we never had enough food to eat and our tiny camper was always such a wreck, but I couldn't tell Eddie that. He was in one of his fighting moods, and he would've given me all kinds of hell if I'd told him what I really thought. It wasn't like he didn't know things were bad. I'd heard him complain many times, but he had a point to make and he damn well was going to make it.

"It's those fucking kids you've been running with. That stuck-up little twat...What's her name? Jae Michaels or something, and that Hughes kid, living large on his daddy's farming money. That got you all twisted up, thinking you're better than us, but you best get this through that pretty little head of yours right now—like it or not, you're not a fucking Michaels or a Hughes. You're a goddamn Harrington, and when your goody-goody buddies figure out who you really are, they'll kick your ass to the curb."

"They aren't like that," I told him as I tried to fight back my tears. "They're my friends."

"Yeah, until they find out that their little friend is nothing more than poor white trash. That she lives in a fucking camper, and her father is a drunk and her mother stays cracked out on coke." He shook his head with disgust. "When they figure that shit out, they'll be long gone. You can count on it."

"Shut the fuck up, Eddie," Danny scolded.

"What?" He shrugged. "You know I'm right."

Before he could start in on me again, I ran outside and got on my bike. As I started to pedal down the old dirt path beside our camper, I thought back over everything Eddie had said. I hated him for it, but deep down, I knew he was right. I'd seen the same thing happen with my brothers' friends. They'd all turned their backs on them, and I knew it was only a matter of time before mine did the same. It was at that moment I decided I wasn't going to let that happen to me. I'd take matters into my own hands and end the friendships myself. I let myself believe that I didn't need them—that I didn't need anybody, but I was wrong.

Over the next few years, things at home got even worse. My father was sent to prison for selling drugs, my brothers were never around, and when they were, it was never good. They were always in trouble for one reason or another, and to top things off, Mom up and left, leaving me to fend for myself. I had no friends or family I could turn to, so I learned really quick—if I wanted to survive in this world, I'd have to do it on my own. That seemed like a lifetime ago. So much had changed since then, and from the looks of it, the same held true for Caleb. The once star quarterback was now a member of one of the most dangerous MCs in the South. I was curious to know how he'd ended up there. It had to be one hell of a story, and I wondered if, in time, he might share it with me.

Rider

The garage had always been a place where the brothers could cut loose and say whatever the hell was on their minds without giving a flying-fuck who was around, but today the guys were being oddly quiet. They were all busy working, and other than a few stray comments, no one had much to say. I figured the silence was because it was Darcy's first day, and the guys were trying to make a good first impression. I couldn't blame them. Darcy wasn't only talented, but beautiful—even more so than I remembered. She still had the same long, auburn hair, crystal blue eyes, and knockout figure, but there was something different about her.

Maybe it was confidence in her work or the fact that she'd grown into a woman. Whatever it was, it looked unbelievably good on her. Darcy wasn't even dolled up, she was simply wearing a pair of green overalls with a white tank and had her hair pulled back in a ponytail, yet I was struggling to keep my eyes off her. I was supposed to be busy finishing up an engine install, but I kept glancing over in her direction, watching as she got everything prepped for her first project—a Harley-Davidson softail. The owner wanted it painted red with a dragon inlay on the gas tank. The bike was decent enough, but once Darcy was finished, it would look incredible.

T-Bone and I had already sandblasted and prepped everything for her, but the pieces needed to be moved and put on the stands in the paint room. Darcy had just picked up the first fender when she tripped on a hose that one of the guys left laying on ground and landed on the ground. She did what she could to brace her fall, but it didn't do much to lessen the impact. I started towards her, but stopped when she quickly sprang to her feet. She looked down at the fender in her hand, and when she noticed her fall had caused a small dent on the lower extension of the fender, she lost it. "Goddamn sonofabitch! I can't believe I did that. Mother...*fucker!*"

The entire garage fell silent as my brothers stopped dead in their tracks and stared over at Darcy. They all seemed shocked that she was cussing like a sailor, especially since she was such a beautiful woman, but they'd soon learn that Darcy Harrington wasn't like most women. She was one of a kind. I watched with curiosity as T-Bone rushed over to her and asked, "You okay, doll?"

"*Doll?* Seriously?" She put her hand on her hip and glared at him with disgust. Damn. If looks could kill, T-Bone would've been nothing but a pile of dust and bones. "Do you call everyone around here *doll?*"

"*No.*" His brows furrowed with confusion. "Can't say that I do."

"I didn't think so." She took a step towards T-Bone, a monster of a man who reminded us all of Mr. Clean, only he was covered in menacing tattoos. Darcy didn't seem to mind at all that he could easily snap her like a twig as she barked, "Let me make this clear...I'm nobody's doll, so you can save that shit for one your club girls."

"Whoa. Hold up," he stammered. "I didn't mean anything by it."

"Maybe not." Her tone softened as she continued, "But if I'm gonna be working here, then I'm gonna need you and everyone else around here to treat me like one of the guys. None of that *doll* shit—or *baby* or *sweetheart* or whatever else you guys might call some chick. You think you can manage that?"

"Sure can"—a smirk crossed his face—"but I hope you know what you're in for."

"I'm sure I can handle it."

With that, she turned and walked away, leaving T-Bone standing there shaking his head. After taking the fender over to one of the empty work stations, Darcy got to work on repairing the dent. Knowing she had lots to get done and fixing that damn dent was holding her up, I decided to go over and see if I could help her out. When I walked up, her back was to me, and she never even looked up when I asked, "You need a hand with that?"

"Thanks, but I've got it."

"I have no doubt that you do." She glanced over her shoulder and a surprised expression crossed her face when she saw that it was me. Her eyes locked on mine. "I thought I could knock that out while you got the primer started on the other fender and frame. It's totally up to you. I just figured it might help keep you from getting behind."

"You're probably right." After studying me for a moment, she asked, "You sure you don't mind?"

"Wouldn't have offered if I did."

"All right then." She stepped to the side and let me take her place in front of the fender. "Thanks, Sport."

Just hearing that old nickname reminded me of the guy I used to be—the guy I'd left behind years ago. My tone was firmer than I'd intended when I replied, "The name's Rider."

"*Rider?*" She turned to face me with her eyebrow cocked high. "That your biker name or something?"

"Yeah, something like that."

"Okay. Good to know." Without skipping a beat, she crossed her arms and said, "It's been awhile. I gotta admit, I was kind of surprised to see you here."

"You know how it goes." I shrugged. "Things happen. People change and all that."

"Yeah, they do." Her eyes drifted over me briefly, then she turned and started for the paint room. "Thanks for the help, *Rider*."

I was surprised that Darcy didn't push and ask questions about my past, but I was relieved that she didn't. That was one conversation that I wasn't in the mood to have. Not today. I quickly turned my attention back to the fender. It only took a few minutes for me to fix the dent, and once I was done, I carried it over to the paint room. After putting it on the table with the others, I went back to my station and got busy finishing up my engine install. I hadn't been working long when Blaze came over with Clay, a potential prospect. I didn't know much about him, other than he was Viper's nephew. His uncle was the president of the Ruthless Sinners, and he and his club had helped us out with a situation with Gus's daughter. Just as the dust was settling and we were preparing to leave Nashville, Viper had asked Gus to take Clay on—hoping that one day Gus would give him the opportunity to prospect for

Satan's Fury. Viper would've had him prospect there with the Sinners, but felt that Clay needed a fresh start—one that was far away from Nashville and all the temptations that had gotten him in trouble. After all that Viper and his brothers had done to help us out, there was no way Gus could refuse.

Thankfully, it looked like Clay had some real potential. He'd only been with us a couple of weeks and was still trying to learn the ropes, but he was hanging in there. There was a good chance that Gus would allow him to prospect, but he still had a lot of work to do. I had a feeling that's why Blaze had brought him over to me. He gave me one of his looks as he said, "I thought Clay might be able to give you a hand today."

"I could definitely use one." I turned to Clay as I asked, "Have you ever installed an engine before?"

"Not by myself, but I've seen it done before."

Most of the grunt work had already been done. The engine was in place and just needed to be reconnected. "That's all right. I'll walk you through it."

"When do you think you'll get this thing wrapped up?" Blaze asked.

"Now that I have some help, I should have it done in a couple of hours."

"Good. I'll let Gallagher know it'll be ready to go this afternoon."

It had been a couple of weeks, and Lewis still hadn't made good on his threats aimed at Kenadee. Riggs was still monitoring the Inner Disciples' every move, but nothing over the past few days had drawn his attention. Hopeful that this whole thing might've blown over, I looked over to Blaze and asked, "Things still good with Kenadee?"

"As far as I can tell they are, but that can change at any minute." He ran his hand over his beard. "I still can't shake the feeling that the bomb's about to drop."

"If it does, we'll be ready," I assured him.

"I sure as hell hope so." He started to walk away as he said, "If you need anything, just give me a shout."

Once Blaze was back in his office, I looked over to Clay. Even though he'd been around for a few weeks, I still hadn't gotten accustomed to his size. He was at least six-eight and was built like a fucking ox, reminding me of one of my linebackers back in high school. With biceps twice the size of mine, he looked like he could take down damn near anyone, but he had one of those pretty-boy faces that made him look soft. When he noticed that I was studying him, he asked, "What do you need me to do?"

"Grab a quarter-inch socket wrench and start securing the bolts to the transmission."

It took him several tries, but he finally managed to get the right wrench and got to work on the transmission. While he was doing that, I started to work on the fuel lines and throttle cables. As I was checking the fuel pressure, I couldn't help but notice that things in the garage were no longer quiet. The radio was back on, and the guys were joking around and telling tall tales as they worked. They didn't seem worried at all about offending Darcy, or anyone else for that matter. I couldn't help but think the change had something to do with Darcy's little encounter with T-Bone. She'd made it clear that she wanted to be treated like one of the guys, and they were taking her at her word. I took a quick glance over in Darcy's direction to see if she'd noticed the change in their behavior and found her busy working, completely oblivious to all the ruckus going on in the rest of the garage.

Knowing I had work of my own to tend to, I turned my attention back to Clay. After I'd made certain that he'd secured the transmission, I put him to work on the air intake manifold. I'd hoped that having an extra set of hands would help get the job done faster, but I quickly realized that wasn't the case. Clay needed a lot of direction, which slowed things down. Thankfully, he was a fast learner. If he kept at it, paid attention, and didn't give up, it wouldn't be long before he could take on some jobs of his own. Once we'd finished with the engine, I lowered the hood, then turned to him and said, "You did good."

"No, I didn't, but I promise I'll do better next time."

"I'm sure you will." I motioned over to Blaze's office. "I'm gonna let him know we're done."

"You need me to do anything else?"

I looked around at all the mess around my station. "It'd be great if you could start cleanings things up a bit."

"You got it."

When I got to Blaze's office, he was on the phone, so I stood in the doorway and waited for him to finish his call. It didn't take long for me to figure out that he was talking with Kenadee. While he wasn't calling her quite as often as before, he still felt the need to check in with her from time to time. Once he felt certain that everything was good with her, he hung up the phone and turned his attention to me. "Is the truck ready?"

"Yep. It's all good to go."

"Great." I didn't miss the unease in his voice when he asked, "How did Clay do?"

"He did okay. He's still got a lot to learn, but he catches on fast," I assured him. "In a couple of weeks, he should be able to start handling some things on his own."

"It sure would be nice to have an extra set of hands around here."

"Yes, it would." The garage was started as a front, used simply to launder the money the club brought in from running guns, but over the past few years it had turned into something more. Business was booming, and Blaze was doing everything in his power to keep the momentum going. That was one of the very reasons we'd hired Darcy. "You need us to take care of anything else before we go?"

"No. That's it for the day."

"Then I'm gonna head out." As I walked out of his office, I said, "I'll see ya back at the clubhouse."

I headed back over to my station and was surprised to see that Clay had it in perfect order. Everything was exactly where it was supposed to be. He'd even moved the truck to the front for the owner to pick up. I thanked him and sent him on his way. After gathering my things, I started for the parking lot and was about to step out the back door but stopped when I heard Darcy shout, "Yeah, baby! That's what I'm talking about."

Curious, I turned around and made my way over to the paint room to see what had her so excited. When I stepped inside, I found Darcy in her oversized white painters suit staring down at the freshly painted gas tank. From where I was standing I couldn't see the design, but if her expression was any indication, I'd say that she'd done an amazing job on it. I walked over to her, and just as I suspected, the dragon design she'd created looked incredible. "Damn, that's awesome."

"You think so?"

"Yeah, I do."

Darcy was practically beaming as she looked up at me and said, "Well, I still need to do another layer of clearcoat, but I think you might be right. It looks pretty damn good."

"It looks better than good." A smile crossed her face as I told her, "It looks amazing."

"Thanks." She started unzipping her painter's suit as she asked, "You done for the day?"

"Yeah. I got everything wrapped up and was about to head out. What about you?"

She shrugged. "I'd like to stay and finish this up, but I got the feeling Blaze is ready for me to call it a day."

"He's gotta pick up Kenadee." I glanced over at the clock on the wall to check the time. "If you really want to stay, I could find something to keep me busy for a couple of hours."

"No, that's okay. I can finish everything in the morning."

"Okay. Suit yourself."

I turned and started towards the door but stopped when Darcy asked, "Hey...you wanna grab a beer or something?"

I turned around and she was out of her painting getup, walking towards me and looking hot as ever. Damn. It would be easy to get all twisted up about her again, but I couldn't let that happen. I had to keep my shit together and remember Darcy wasn't just some girl I used to lust over. She was working for the club now, and I couldn't fuck that up. Noticing my hesitation, she nudged me with her elbow. "Come on, Rider. It's just a beer. I'm not asking you to walk down the aisle."

Darcy

I don't know what possessed me to ask Caleb to go out for a beer. Maybe I wanted to celebrate the fact that I'd survived my first day at the Satan's Fury garage or maybe it was the simple fact that I wanted to reconnect with an old friend. There was a time when Caleb and I were close, *really close*. We told each other everything, finished each other's sentences. Hell, I knew what he was thinking even before he did, but that was a long time ago. Looking at him now, I had no idea what was going on in that head of his, but it was clear that he had his reservations about going out to have a drink with me. I won't deny that the realization stung a bit. I was beginning to think he was going to turn me down when he finally asked, "Where do you want to go to have this beer?"

"I'm not picky." I shrugged. "You decide."

"We could go over to the 8-Ball. It's just around the corner."

"Sounds good to me." I walked over and grabbed my wallet and keys off the table. "I'm ready when you are."

I followed him out to the parking lot, and after we'd

both gotten on our bikes, we drove over to the 8-Ball. The place was pretty empty, just a couple of old dudes playing a game of pool and two more up at the counter, so we didn't have any trouble finding a spot to sit. We'd just gotten settled when the bartender shouted from across the room, "Hey, you two...what will it be?"

"Two beers," Caleb answered. "Whatever you have on tap."

"You got it."

Caleb and I sat there in awkward silence while we waited for our beers to be brought over. As soon as he'd placed them down on the table, we both reached for our glasses and took a long drink, then Caleb broke the ice by asking, "So, what's with the crotch-rocket?"

"I'll have you know, that crotch-rocket is an amazing piece of machinery," I sassed. "It'll take a right-hand curve at eighty miles an hour like it's gliding across glass."

"Um-hmm. It's still a crotch-rocket," he scoffed.

"It's a Kawasaki H2R." I took another sip of my beer before asking, "Have you ever even ridden on one?"

"No. Can't say that I have."

"Well, you know what they say. Don't knock it till you try it."

"What about you? Ever ridden on a Harley?"

"A couple of times." I shrugged. "They're cool and all, but if you ask me, they're overrated."

"I'm gonna pretend you didn't just say that."

I chuckled as I said, "I'm just telling it like I see it."

"You keep talking shit, and I'm gonna need another beer," he fussed.

"Okay, I'll ease up on you." I smiled as I watched him take a tug off his beer. "Hey...you remember back when we were kids, how we'd spend every recess trying to see who could swing the highest? I'd beat you every single time."

"Funny. That's not how I remember it at all." His lips curled into a sexy smirk as he continued, "But I'll tell you this—if you did happen to win on some rare occasion, it's because I let you. The same goes for those races across the soccer field."

"You are so full of shit!" I gasped. "I won those races fair and square, and you know it!"

He shrugged. "If you say so."

"Whatever. I know who won."

"I do, too. It was *me*." When Caleb saw my mouth drop, he shook his head and snickered. "You always were a sore loser."

"Maybe so, but that's only because I didn't get much practice with it," I argued, "'cause I was *always winning*."

"Um-hmm. Whatever helps you sleep at night." Again, I gasped. Seeing that he'd gotten the reaction he was looking for, he decided to try and change the subject. "Do you remember how Mrs. Collins was always on our ass about being late?"

"I know what you did there...changed the subject before I had a chance to prove you wrong, but I'll let it slide this time." I took another drink of my beer before I smiled and answered, "Mrs. Collins was an uptight, crabby old biddy who needed to get laid."

"I don't disagree with you there. She was a fucking killer when she brought out that damn paddle." He shook his head and winced. "I don't think my ass was ever the same after she got me that last time."

Even though I knew exactly which time he was referring to, I didn't know all the details behind it so I asked,

"You talking about that day when you and Ethan Taylor got into it in sixth grade?"

"That would be it."

"I thought so. Mrs. Collins was fuming when she broke you two up." Hoping for some clarification, I asked, "I can't remember. What did you two fight about anyway?"

"Hell, I can't really remember." It was clear from his expression and tone of voice that he was lying, which made me wonder if their argument had something to do with me. "But if I had to guess, I'd say he was running his mouth about something, and I got tired of hearing it."

From day one, Caleb was one of the most popular boys in school, but he never let it go to his head. If he saw a weaker kid getting bullied, he would always jump in to give them a hand. It's just the kind of guy he was, and one of the many reasons why everyone thought so much of him. I smiled slightly and said, "Ethan was a douchebag."

"Yes, he was," Caleb agreed. "But I shouldn't have decked him like I did...at least not during the middle of Mrs. Collins's class. I should've at least waited until she wasn't in the front of the room teaching."

"You're probably right," I scoffed. "Maybe then, she wouldn't have gotten so pissed about it."

"I doubt it would've made much difference. She was always looking for someone to crawl." He chuckled to himself as he reached into his pocket for his cigarettes. As he lit one, he looked over to me and asked, "So, how did a girl from the small town of Oakland learn to paint the way you do?"

"I don't know." I gave him a slight shrug. "It was just something I kind of picked up."

"How did you get started?"

I thought back for a moment, then replied, "I'm not sure if you remember that old pickup I had?"

"Yeah, I remember it."

"Then, you know it was in pretty rough shape." He nodded, and I continued, "I wanted to see what I could do with it, so I tried anything I could get my hands on, which wasn't much. I didn't have any money at the time, so it was mainly second-rate spray paint, but it actually turned out fairly decent. A couple of my brothers' friends paid me to work on some of their stuff, and it wasn't long before I was able to buy some basic equipment."

"So, no one taught you how to do it?"

"I took art in high school and learned some basics, but for the most part, no, I taught myself." I shrugged. "With each new job, I tried different things, created more intricate designs and colors, and eventually figured out how to do it like the bigger shops."

"That's really incredible, Darcy." When I saw the way Caleb was looking at me, so intense and genuine, a delicious shiver ran down my spine. I knew I should look away, but my traitorous eyes remained locked on his. It was like I was under some kind of spell, but thankfully, his gaze eventually dropped to the table and the moment was broken. "You should be really proud of what you've accomplished."

"I've done okay. I'm just hoping this new position at your club's garage was a good move." Dread crept over me like an icy chill at just the thought of everything I'd worked for going up in smoke. Even though Fury had made a name for themselves and people from all over were trying to get their vehicles into their garage, there was no way of knowing how things were going to play out, especially with the members. I was hopeful, but I knew from past experiences, that things rarely go the way I expected them to. I looked over to Caleb and said, "I took a big risk leaving Thompson's like I did."

"If it makes you feel any better, I think you made the right decision." His expression softened, and I could hear the sincerity in his voice. "They'll look out for you and help out any way they can. Each and every one of them."

"I don't need them or anyone else looking out for me, Rider."

He cocked his eyebrow at me as he gave me a look that had me shifting in my seat. "Someone having your back isn't a bad thing, Darcy."

"No. Not until the day they aren't there when you really need them. That's when you realize you can't really depend on anyone but yourself."

I could tell by his expression that he wasn't expecting my response, so I wasn't surprised when he asked, "What makes you say that?"

"Because it's true. At least, it was for me." I lifted my beer and finished it off before I continued, "Things at home had never been good for me or my brothers, but the day Mom walked out on us, things got even worse. Dad was already in jail. Danny and Eddie did what they could, but they kept getting into trouble with the law, too. That's when I learned I had to survive on my own, or not at all."

His eyes darkened with sympathy as he whispered, "I'm sorry things were so tough for you."

"There's nothing for you to feel sorry for. I'm sitting here right now, living and breathing. I've done okay for myself, so just save your sympathy for someone else."

"Damn, Darcy." Caleb leaned back and crossed his arms, giving me one of those looks that made me wish I'd kept my thoughts to myself. "If you put those walls up any higher, no one's gonna get in or out, including you."

"How would you know? Are you speaking from experience, Mr. I-grew-up-with-a-silver-spoon-in-my-mouth?"

"You don't know me as well as you think you do."

"I know you grew up with two parents who loved you and your sister, and they made sure you had food on the table and clothes on your back."

There was no missing the pain in his voice as he said, "Yeah, but when things went south, they kicked my ass to the curb, turned their backs on me, and as far as I know, they never looked back."

"I didn't know they did that to you."

"It wasn't like I gave them much choice in the matter. Hell, I would've done the same fucking thing if I was in their shoes." His eyes skirted to the floor, and suddenly it felt like he was a hundred miles away. I wanted to reach out and comfort him in some way, make him forget about whatever was weighing on him, but I just sat there and listened as he said, "I was a complete mess after the accident."

Everybody in Oakland and three counties over had heard about the star quarterback who had almost lost his arm in the cotton picker, but I never knew how it happened. It couldn't be easy for him to talk about, so I hesitated to ask him. Thankfully, I didn't have to. After several minutes, he started, "I'd been sitting in the cab, letting the engine warm up, and was just about to go out into the field, when I heard this strange noise coming from the picker. I'd gotten out to see what it was and noticed that some spindles were hitting the head cover."

"I'm guessing that's a bad thing."

"Well, it's not good but could easily be fixed, I just

couldn't do it alone. I was about to get back up in the cab to kill the engine when it happened." His face twisted into a pained grimace. "I don't even know how it did, but my sleeve had gotten caught and my arm was pulled into the spindles."

"Oh, God. You're lucky you didn't lose your arm."

"I would've, if I hadn't managed to pull it free, but I still fucked it up pretty badly."

"How bad was it?"

"I was cut up pretty badly, torn muscle and tendons, and my wrist was dislocated. I ended up being airlifted to Vanderbilt. The muscles were damaged, so the surgeon there had to take some from my back and transplant them into my forearm." It was difficult to hear about everything that had happened to him. I could only imagine how hard it must have been to actually live through it. Caleb let out a deep sigh as he lifted his arm and clenched his fist. "Thankfully, they were able to repair the tendons and restore function to my arm and hand, but my football days were over."

"Everybody said you were the best quarterback who'd ever come through Oakland." I could still remember the times I'd seen him play. The crowd loved him. They were always cheering him on and shouting his praises. "It must've been really hard to accept that you couldn't play anymore."

"Yeah. That was the hardest part of all of it." He shook his head. "I didn't see the point of doing all that damn physical therapy if I wasn't ever gonna throw a ball again, so I eventually stopped going. I was all fucked up in the head. I closed myself off and started downing my pain meds like they were Tic Tacs. It wasn't long before I found myself in a dark place...*a very dark place.*"

Rider

My addiction to painkillers wasn't just about the high. It was the overwhelming need to find an escape. The accident had not only stolen my ability to play football, but it'd also stolen my identity. I had no idea who I was anymore. I felt empty, with no direction or purpose, and I hated myself for it. With each day that passed, the darkness inside of me grew stronger to the point where I was fucking drowning in it. Instead of reaching out for help, I'd just swallow another pill...and then another. When the doctors stopped filling my scripts, I found myself searching through my friends' and family's medicine cabinets. I'd steal whatever pain meds I could get my hands on. It took my folks several months to figure out what was going on, but once they finally did, they became desperate to help me get back on track. They tightened the reins, monitored my every move, and when that didn't work, they'd sent me to a counselor in hopes that he could help put an end to my addiction. They just didn't get it though. My need to forget the anger and resentment I'd felt for losing my one chance to get out of Oakland had taken its toll, and I was determined to find my next fix. No counselor was going to change that.

"After going through what you did, no one could blame you for winding up in such a dark place."

"Don't try to justify it. There's no excuse for the things I did, Darcy."

"You were hurting," she replied softly. "Not just physically, but mentally."

"Yeah, but I should've sucked it up and moved on. Instead, I wallowed in self-pity and hurt the people I cared about most."

"It wasn't like you set out to hurt them."

"No, but I did so just the same."

I could still remember the look of horror on my parents' faces when they discovered that I'd not only hocked my grandmother's wedding ring, but also my mother's earrings so I could buy more pills. On that same day, they found out that I'd completely wiped out my college fund. Maybe it wouldn't have been so bad if I hadn't stolen from them before, but by then, they'd had enough and kicked me out.

My old buddy, Bryce, was going to college at Memphis State, so I went to stay with him for a while. Unfortunately, with no job and an endless addiction, it didn't take long for me to wear out my welcome, and he sent me packing. I hit up another friend and then another, but the results were always the same. Eventually, I found myself strung out and living on the streets. It wasn't something I was proud of. Hell, I hated myself for letting things get so fucking bad. It took almost freezing to death one night in the snow for me to realize that it was time to make a change.

I was lost in my own head when Darcy placed her hand

on my knee and said, "We all make mistakes, Caleb. We just have to learn from them and move on. From what I can see, you've done that."

"I've definitely tried."

"That's all anyone can ask for." Darcy removed her hand from my thigh as she looked up at me with warm smile. "This might not be the life you were planning on, but it seems like you've done pretty well for yourself."

"I like to think so."

A spark of mischief crossed her eyes as she announced, "I do have *one* question for you."

"Okay. Shoot."

"After everything that happened, how'd you end up with Satan's Fury?"

I finished off my beer, then stood up. "That, my dear, is a story for another day."

Without arguing, she followed me out the door and to the parking lot. We'd just walked up on our bikes when she turned to me and said, "You could at least tell me where the name Rider came from?"

"Yeah, I could, but I'm not." I threw my leg over the seat of my Harley. "Where you headed?"

"Home."

"All right then. Lead the way."

Darcy's brows furrowed as she asked, "What do you mean, 'lead the way'?"

"I mean exactly that," I answered flatly. "I'm going to make sure you get home okay."

"I'm a big girl, Rider," she fussed. "I can make it home without a chaperone."

"I'm sure you can, but I'm following you home just the same."

A determined look crossed her face as she slipped on

her helmet. "Fine. Follow me if you want to, but you're going to have to keep up."

With that, she hopped on her bike and started the engine. I knew I was in trouble the second she pulled out of the parking lot. Darcy never let off the gas as she whipped out into traffic, leaving me in her wake. Cursing like a madman, I tried to catch up to her, but she was already several blocks ahead of me. Hammering down on the accelerator, I tried to catch up to the yellow blur ahead of me, but lost all my momentum when I got stopped by a red light. Just like that, she vanished off into the distance. Refusing to let her get the best of me, I pulled over and called Riggs at the clubhouse. As soon as he answered, I told him, "I need Darcy Harrington's address."

"That the new painter Blaze just hired?"

"Yeah, that's her."

There was no missing the curiosity in his voice when he asked, "There a particular reason why you need her address?"

"We went to grab a beer after work, and I just wanted to make sure she made it home okay."

"Why didn't you just follow her home?"

I sighed as I answered, "I tried."

"*Oh*. Well then...just give me a minute." As the club's computer hacker, Riggs had a way of finding things that no one else could, so there wasn't a doubt in my mind that he'd be able to track down Darcy's address. Just as I'd hoped, he came back to the phone and said, "Got it. She lives at Thirty-two Shady Pines in Millington."

"Shady Pines?"

"Yeah. I'm pretty sure it's a trailer park for the retired. Any idea why she'd be living there?"

"Got no idea, but I'm about to find out."

I hung up, then shoved my phone into my back pocket and started towards Shady Pines. It was about a thirty-minute drive out to her place, but with the way she drove, I had no doubt that she'd gotten there much faster. Not long after I entered the park, I spotted her yellow crotch-rocket parked at the end of the lot next to one of the older trailers. It was pale yellow with flowers planted at the mailbox, and a small white awning covering the wooden deck that led up to the front door. As I got closer, I noticed her old pickup truck from high school was also parked in the driveway. What used to look like an old clunker held together by rust was now painted candy-apple red with a sweet black trim. I pulled up next to it, and once I was parked, I killed the engine and removed my helmet. I was just about to start up her front steps when I heard a woman call out to me. "Well, hello there, young man."

I looked to my left and found two elderly ladies, both reminding me of Aunt Bee from the *Andy Griffith Show*, sitting on the front porch of a neighboring trailer. I smiled at them both as answered, "Hello, ladies. How are you doing tonight?"

"We're doing just fine." The lady in the bright-yellow "old lady" dress with a front zipper and slip-on house shoes lifted her glass. "We're having ourselves a little nightcap."

"Is that right?" I chuckled. "Well, it's a nice night for one."

"*Um-hmm.* We thought so." She lowered her glasses down the bridge of her nose as she gave me a quick once over. "Haven't seen you around here before. Are you a friend of Darcy's?"

"Yes, ma'am. I guess you could say that."

"Well, you sure are a handsome fellow." She gave her

friend a little nudge as she asked, "Don't you think so, Frances?"

"I sure do. I think he is very handsome indeed." She nodded and smiled so wide, I thought her dentures might fall out. "If I was a might younger, I'd go after a fella like him. I sure would, and I'd show him a *real good time*."

"Um-hmm." With a humorous smile and a shake of her head, the friend replied, "I'm sure you would."

"Well, I'm going to let you ladies get back to your drinks." Fearing what they might say next, I told them, "I'm going to check in on Darcy. You two enjoy your night."

"You too, handsome."

I could feel their eyes burning a hole in me as I started up the steps. Once I got up to the door, I knocked and waited for Darcy to answer. After several loud thuds and bangs, the door flew open and the air rushed from my lungs when I found Darcy standing there in nothing but a white wife-beater tank top and a pair of black lace panties. Her long hair was pulled back away from her face, revealing her gorgeous blue eyes and the tiny freckles on the bridge of her nose. I couldn't have dreamed up a more beautiful sight, and the look of absolute surprise on her face only made her that much more irresistible when she gasped. "What are you doing here?"

"I told you," I shrugged, playing off my intrusion, "I wanted to see that you made it home okay."

"Yeah, but how did you know where I lived?"

"You gotta remember who you're working for."

I could see the wheels turning in her head before she replied, "I didn't give my home address on my application. I used my PO Box."

"Like I said, you've gotta remember who you're working for."

"Damn, I don't know if I should be impressed or pissed off as all hell."

Darcy was still glaring at me as I took a step back and casually looked around her place. It was an okay place, but there were several things that needed work. Some of the boards on her porch had buckled and the nails were exposed, the light beside her front door was busted, and the chain lock on her door no longer had a chain. There was literally nothing to keep someone from breaking in on her. That bothered me the most. As I stared down at her door, I said, "You don't have a lock on your front door."

"Yeah. I've been meaning to fix that."

"And you don't have any cameras or an alarm."

She shrugged as she replied, "Nope. Sure don't."

"The lighting isn't all that great either."

Her hands dropped to her hips, and she gave me an angry scowl as she snapped, "The lighting is just fine, and I don't need a deadbolt, security cameras, or alarms. I have Thelma and Louise living next door. They're all the security I need."

"Thelma and Louise are almost eighty years old, Darcy. How the hell are they going—"

"They watch this place like a hawk. Hell, there's nothing that goes on here that those two don't know about." She cocked her eyebrow and snickered. "I bet they noticed you the second you pulled up here."

There was something about that determined tone in her voice that stirred something deep inside of me, and if I wasn't careful, I would end up doing something I might regret. Knowing I was fighting a battle I couldn't win, I shook my head and said, "Fine. I won't say another word."

"Good." She opened the door further. "Do you want to come in, or are you going to stay out there all night?"

I stepped inside and told her, "I can't stay long."

"I take it you've gotta get back to the clubhouse."

"I do."

"Figured as much." She turned, and as she started to saunter down the hall, I couldn't stop myself from staring in awe at her perfect ass as it peaked through the edges of her barely-there black lace panties. Fuck. I'd never seen a hotter sight. The girl was killing me. I needed to get a fucking grip. I was still staring down the hall even after she disappeared into her bedroom and shouted, "Give me just a second."

"Take your time."

I used the moment alone to check out her place. I was pleasantly surprised to see that the inside of her trailer was in much better shape than the outside. It was small but comfortable, with a tiny kitchen that was connected to her living room. The furniture was sparse, but what she had was nice. I could tell that she'd put a lot of work into making it something she could be proud of. I was still standing at the front door when Darcy returned wearing a pair of oversized sweats, but the vision of her in those black panties was burned into my brain. Hoping to shake the memory from my mind, I asked, "How long have you been living at Shady Pines?"

"I moved in about two years ago." She walked over next to me and leaned against the kitchen counter. "I was looking for a place of my own, and this was something I could actually afford. I mean, I have to do a little work here and there, but it's worth it."

"Sounds like you have a sweet deal going here."

"I guess so." Her nose crinkled into a grimace as she

said, "As much as I like being here, I'd really like to find a place closer to work."

"I'm sure your lady friends next door will miss you when you go."

"Maybe, but those two will make it just fine no matter what."

I glanced down at my watch, and when I noticed the time, I told her, "I better get going."

"Okay."

Earlier, I'd noticed a small dry erase board on her fridge with a marker attached. Before I headed for the door, I walked over and wrote the number to my burner cell on the board. Once I was done, I turned back to her and said, "If something comes up that Thelma and Louise can't handle, just give me a call."

"I'll do that," she scoffed, as she followed me over to the door. "Be careful heading back."

"Will do." I went down the steps and walked over to my bike. "I'll see you in the morning."

She gave me a quick wave, then stepped back into her trailer, closing the door. I'd just swung a leg over my Harley when my burner started to ring. I grabbed it out of my back pocket, and as soon as I answered, Shadow asked, "You still at Darcy's place?"

"Yeah, but I'm heading out. Why?"

"We had some trouble with Kenadee tonight. Gonna need you to get back to the clubhouse as soon as you can."

"I'm on my way." Before I hung up, I asked, "Is Kenadee okay?"

"Yeah, she's okay. We've just gotta make sure she stays that way."

Darcy

❦

I can't remember a time when I'd been more surprised by a man's actions than I was when Caleb showed up at my door—and that's saying something. I was rarely surprised by men or their actions, not after all I'd seen over the years, but Caleb got me. After I'd lost him at that red light, I figured he would've just given up and gone on about his business, but I couldn't have been more wrong. The man was determined to make a point, and he damn well made it. I tried to play it cool, but it wasn't easy, especially with the way he was staring at me with those sexy, brooding eyes. It didn't help matters that he looked unbelievably hot in his black leather cut and tattered jeans. I didn't know what to do with myself. I hadn't been around someone I was interested in for quite some time. In fact, it had been over a year since I'd been out with a guy—and that was nothing memorable—nothing like the time I'd just spent with Caleb.

I wasn't sure if I'd ever enjoyed myself as much as I had with him at the bar. It felt so good to get reacquainted with Caleb again. With each moment we spent together, I found myself wanting to get to know him even better, but unfortunately, that couldn't happen. I needed to keep my distance. Maybe if the circumstances weren't what they were, and I hadn't just started working at the garage, needing to keep my focus, then maybe things could've been different. That didn't mean I'd never gone to bed and spent half the night thinking about him—because I had, especially that night he'd come to my rescue. We were supposed to meet up for a date the following evening but, because of his accident, that never happened. It was impossible not to wonder what might've happened if he'd actually made it that night. Sadly, I'd never know.

The following morning, I got up and headed to work. When I arrived at the garage, I was surprised to find that there weren't many guys working. No Rider. No Blaze or Shadow. Other than a few guys who I hadn't really met before, the place was pretty empty. Curious to see what was up, I asked one of the guys who was actually there working, "Hey, where is everyone?"

He was bent over the hood so I couldn't see much of his face, but he was tall and slender with tattoos covering both his arms. Never looking up, he answered, "Not coming in today."

"Why not?" I pushed.

"Club business."

"What kind of club business?"

He turned and looked over his shoulder as he spat, "The kind of club business you don't talk about with anyone not wearing a fucking patch."

"Fine, I get it." I held up my hands in surrender. "I was just asking."

"Well, don't." His eyes narrowed with annoyance as he

motioned his head towards the paint room. "Don't you have some work you need to get to?"

"Yeah, actually I do."

Before he could say anything more, I turned and started back towards my paint room. I was curious about what kind of club business would've pulled them all from work, especially when they were so busy, but it was clear that I wouldn't be getting any answers any time soon. Thankfully, I had a ton of work to do, so there wasn't much time to fixate on what was going on. I finished putting the clear-coat on the bike I'd been working on and moved to the next. In a matter of a few hours, I'd added a base coat to the 1941 Harley WLDR race bike I'd just started and was preparing to start on the gas tank. I had to admit, it was a sweet ride for a Harley, and I was excited to see how awesome it looked with the deep royal-blue undercoat. When I noticed the other guys were packing up for the day, I knew it was almost closing time, so I decided to put off the tank-detailing until tomorrow. I cleaned up my station, removed my painting garb, and grabbed my keys. On my way out the back door, I shouted, "See you guys tomorrow."

"Have a safe trip home," one of them answered.

"Will do."

A few hours of daylight still remained, so I took my time riding home. The weather was starting to change, and autumn's cool air was setting in. The leaves had just begun to change colors, with just the tips becoming a bright shade of yellow or red, and each time the wind blew, the acorns and pecans would fall from the trees. As much as I loved this time of year, I knew it wouldn't be long before winter came creeping in. The temps would drop and the roads would become sketchy, making it difficult to ride my bike to work. The bitter weather was one of the reasons I'd held on to the old pickup truck—that, and it was the only thing I'd ever gotten from my grandfather in my entire life. I was lucky he'd passed it on to me. By the time he died, there wasn't a dime left to his name, and it took all the money my brothers and I had saved to bury him. I was still thinking about the day we'd put him in the ground as I pulled up to my trailer. After I parked and started to get off my bike, I noticed Ms. Maybell was trying to take potted mums out of the trunk of her car.

Ms. Maybell had to be in her late seventies, but with her smooth dark skin and shiny dark-black hair, she looked much younger. The only thing that gave her age away was the fact that she moved very slowly, especially when lifting anything that weighed more than a couple of pounds. Worried she might hurt herself, I rushed over and pulled one of the pots out of her trunk. "Can I give you a hand with those?"

"Oh, honey. You don't have to do that."

A few weeks ago, I'd overheard Frances and Alice talking about Maybell and how she'd recently lost one of her great-grandkids. She'd taken the whole thing pretty hard. I couldn't really blame her. Apparently, the kid had gotten caught up in some crossfire between rival gangs, and by the time they got him to the hospital, it was too late. It made me wish I could do more for her than simply put out a few flowers. I gave her a smile as I asked, "Where do you want this one?"

"Over on that front step would be nice, don't you think?"

"Yes, ma'am. I sure do." I placed it on the bottom step next to the railing, then went back to the trunk to grab another. "How about this one?"

"I think that one should go up on the porch by the door."

"You got it."

I had just made my way up the steps when I heard a car pull up in front of Maybell's trailer. I turned to look and was surprised to see KeShawn getting out of his black Mercedes. He was shaking his head as he fussed at Maybell. "I told you I would help you put those out, Mimi."

"I know, but Darcy came over and offered to help."

He reached into the trunk and grabbed another one of the mums as he scolded, "You shouldn't have her out here doing this sort of thing for you."

"I don't mind." I placed the mum by the door then turned and started back down the steps. "I like helping. Besides, Maybell would do it for me if she could."

His tone softened as he said, "I appreciate you looking after her like you do."

"We look out for each other." KeShawn was putting on a show for his grandmother. I knew who he really was—the leader of the Inner Disciples. He was a man who made a living off of the weak, never caring who he hurt to get what he wanted. Men like him were a dime a dozen in the city, and I'd always done my best to steer clear of them. Unfortunately, I hadn't been able to do that with KeShawn. He was always coming around, sometimes alone and sometimes with his crew, to see about Maybell. Normally, I'd just stay out of sight whenever he showed up, but I had no idea he'd stop by today. I smiled at Maybell as I lifted the last pot of mums out of her trunk. "How about this one?"

"I don't know," Maybell answered. "What do you think?"

"I think it would look great on the table by your swing. What do you think about that?"

"I think that will be just perfect, dear," Maybell answered excitedly. "They all look so beautiful, don't they, KeShawn?"

"Yeah. They look real nice, Mimi."

I figured Maybell would like some time alone with her grandson, so I gave them both a quick wave and said, "I hope you two have a nice visit."

When I started to step away, KeShawn called out to me. "Hey, you still painting bikes and shit?"

"Yeah." I stopped and turned to face him. "Why?"

"I've got this sweet Suzuki GSX-R that needs some work. I was thinking you might look at it and give me a price on blacking it out."

"Sure. I could do that. You can bring it by sometime or I can come out to your place and check it out," I offered, praying that he wouldn't take me up on it.

"It's over on Broad Street." He pulled a card out of his wallet with his number on it and brought it over to me. "Just come by when you get a chance. If I'm not around, tell the boys why you're there."

As I took the card from his hand, I nodded. "I'll try to get there in the next week or so."

"Sounds good."

"I wanted to tell you..." I started but hesitated, fearing I might be crossing a line. Unfortunately, I'd already opened my mouth, and he was standing there waiting for me to finish. "I was really sorry to hear about your son."

"Thanks, I appreciate that." A pained expression crossed his face. "Nothing worse than losing a kid, especially one as awesome as Little T."

"I'd seen him a couple of times when he came to visit Maybell. He seemed like he was a great kid."

"He was, and it wasn't right that he went out like he did." He looked up at me with nothing but rage in his eyes as he growled, "That's why I'm gonna make 'em pay...every last one of them."

Knowing that KeShawn was a member of a vicious gang in the city and wouldn't make a threat like that unless he meant it, I suddenly became nervous. I had no idea how to respond to him, so I simply said, "I understand why you might feel that way, but it won't bring him back."

"No, but it'll teach those motherfuckers a lesson. You don't fuck around with me or mine without paying the price."

It was starting to get dark, and I was feeling more uncomfortable by the second, so I nodded. "Well, I better get going. I hope you and Maybell have a nice visit."

With that, I turned towards my trailer. As I started up the steps, I heard Maybell call out to me. "Thank you again for your help, sweet child."

"Anytime!"

The second I stepped up on the porch, I noticed that the light outside my door was not only on and working, it was much brighter than it had been before. I also noticed that several of the loose boards on my porch had been replaced. When I turned to ask Maybell if she'd seen anyone working on my place, I found KeShawn staring at me. There was something about his expression that gave me the creeps, so I rushed inside and quickly closed the door behind me. Relieved to be away from the madness that was KeShawn, I went over to the fridge to get me something to eat. That's when I spotted Caleb's number written on the dry erase board. Curious if he had something to do with my newly repaired light, I took out my phone and sent him a text.

ME: HEY. IT'S DARCY. WOULD YOU HAPPEN TO KNOW anything about my front porch or the backdoor light?

CALEB: MAYBE.

ME: YOU DON'T HAVE TIME TO COME TO WORK, BUT YOU make time to come over and fix my porch?

CALEB: NEEDED TO BE DONE.

ME: I COULD'VE DONE IT MYSELF.

CALEB: MAYBE. BUT YOU DIDN'T.

BEFORE I HAD A CHANCE TO TYPE A RESPONSE, HE messaged again:

Caleb: Good night, Darcy.

ME: GOOD NIGHT.

FEELING FRUSTRATED, I DECIDED TO SKIP DINNER

altogether. I fed Scout and Lenny, then went to take a much needed shower. Once I was done, I put on a t-shirt and crashed on my bed. As I laid there staring up at the ceiling, my mind drifted to Caleb. I found myself wondering what kind of business would've kept him gone not for just a couple of hours, but for the entire day. I had a feeling I might never find out. In fact, I had a feeling that when it came to Caleb and his brothers, there were going to be many things that I would be left in the dark about—and I wasn't sure how I felt about that.

Rider

***

"Like I said before, I told the guy to back the fuck off," Gauge started, "and that Kenadee was an ol' lady and under Fury's protection, and if anyone fucked with her, there'd be hell to pay."

"You gotta know that he went back and told KeShawn about your encounter," Riggs added.

"No doubt." Shadow leaned back in his chair and crossed his arms. "I'm sure he wasn't happy about the news."

"I don't know, brother. I got the feeling the guy already knew." Gauge cocked his head to the side. "He had no reaction whatsoever when I mentioned Fury's name. Hell, he didn't even blink, much less back away."

"Fuck that shit," T-Bone roared. "That motherfucker will blink when I put a goddamn bullet between his eyes."

"You're right about that."

"If Lewis was smart, he'd back the fuck off and let this thing die." Murphy shook his head as he continued, "But I've got a feeling he's going to take it all the way."

There was no missing the rage in Blaze's voice when he

declared, "I've got the same fucking feeling, and I'm telling you right fucking now, I'll kill every last one of them before I let them get to Kenadee."

"We're not going to let anything happen to Kenadee," Gus assured him. "If the Disciples don't heed Gauge's warning, then we'll take action. I know it isn't easy. I know you want to go in there and wipe these fuckers out, but right now, a threat in a moment of grief doesn't justify killing off a hundred men and their families."

"But one of his guys was at the hospital, and he was following Kenadee! That's gotta mean something!"

Dealing with our local city street gangs was a pain in the ass. There was nothing organized about them. Hell, they were dispersed all over their fucking territory. More than half of them slept late and spent the rest of their day hanging around their neighborhood drinking, doping, and causing bullshit trouble. It was pathetic. Not a fucking one of them seemed to be working towards a common goal, and their respect for one another laid in the crimes they committed—the more violent, the more notoriety a member earned, meaning Lewis had to pull some pretty heavy shit to become the leader of the Inner Disciples. Every move his crew made had been driven by his obsession with his turf, his pride, or getting his revenge. There was no doubt that the need to avenge his son's death was fueling Lewis, making him think he had what it took to take us on. Unfortunately for him, it would soon be an emotion that brought him to his end. Gus's tone remained calm as he replied, "And Gauge set the kid straight. Now we wait and see what their next move is gonna be."

Waiting was never easy, especially for a man like Blaze, but in all the years that he'd been our president, Gus had never once let his brothers down. Deep down, Blaze had to know that this time would be no different. With a heavy sigh, Blaze nodded and agreed. "Understood."

"Riggs will continue to monitor the security systems at all their hangouts, but let's step things up a bit." Gus turned to Shadow. "I want you on KeShawn. See if you can figure out if this guy is up to something."

"You got it," Shadow replied.

"Riggs, I need eyes on KeShawn's place at all times. Considering that neighborhood, it won't be easy."

"I'll make it happen."

"I'm gonna hold you to that." Then he turned to Murphy and said, "Until Riggs gets those cameras going, I want you and Rider to go over to keep an eye on KeShawn's. Make sure no one new is going in or coming out of there that we don't know about."

Murphy cocked his eyebrow as he asked, "You want them knowing we're watching?"

"Absolutely."

Murphy nodded. "Understood."

"What about the run to Little Rock in the morning?" Riggs asked.

We had a pipeline with several fellow chapters of Satan's Fury, where each of us contributed to a large shipment of weapons that would be distributed and sold for a prime price. As a whole, we'd made a great deal of money over the past year, but we still continued to complete our own separate runs from time to time, distributing small shipments of handguns or assault rifles. With all that had been going on at the garage and with Kenadee, I'd almost forgotten about the run to Arkansas. Thankfully, it had been planned for weeks. Everything was already crated and ready. It was just a matter of us getting it delivered.

"Murphy will still be in charge." Gus glanced back over

to Murphy once again as he ordered, "You and Rider go by KeShawn's tonight, and then head over there again tomorrow when you get back from the run."

"You got it."

"Before you leave out, I'm gonna need you boys to look over everything and make sure we're set for the morning. Check every single crate and all the artillery," Gus demanded. "Just because this is one of our smaller runs doesn't make it any less of a priority."

We all nodded.

"I'm sending Clay along with you boys tomorrow. It's time to see if he has what it takes to keep up." Gus turned to me as he said, "Rider, watch him. Make sure he doesn't fuck up."

"Yes, sir. I'll do my best."

As soon as church was dismissed, Murphy and I drove to the south of downtown, just past Orange Mound—a territory that was infamous for its plethora of gangs and violence. Knowing how dangerous it could be, most folks did their best to steer clear of this particular neighborhood, especially at night, but we weren't worried. The brothers of Satan's Fury had made a name for themselves, and even downtown with the thugs and thieves, we were protected by our cut. People knew who we were. They knew the kind of destruction we could bring if anyone stood in our way, the wrath that would ensue if they went after one of our own, so we rolled up into that place like we owned it. Murphy and I parked in the wide open space across the street from KeShawn's house, leaving no doubt as to why we were there. There wasn't much to the place, just an old white colonial with four or five bedrooms, sitting right in the middle of the hood. There were lawn chairs scattered around the yard and an old, rusted, fifty-five-gallon metal drum they used as a fire pit. We sat there for over two hours, just watching as some of their guys came and went, but nothing particularly unusual happened the entire time we were there. When it looked like they were closing things down for the night, we waited another hour to be sure, then headed home ourselves.

The following morning, we met up at the clubhouse with the others and started preparing for the run. Like all the times before, we'd hidden the crates in a secret compartment beneath the flooring of Gus's old horse trailers. He'd had them altered years ago when they first started hauling weapons across state lines, and luckily, no one had ever been the wiser. I was watching as T-Bone double checked the compartments when I heard Murphy shout, "Let's move it, boys. We're wasting daylight!"

"One more minute," T-Bone shouted in return. Moments later he came barreling out of the backend of the horse trailer. "I'm done. You can load the horses."

I nodded, then led the horses, one by one, up the ramp and into the trailer. Once I had the door secured, I announced, "We're all set."

"Then, let's roll!" Murphy shouted as he started towards his SUV. He, T-Bone, and Gauge loaded up in his SUV, while Gunner tagged along with Riggs and two of our prospects, Rip and Gash. I was just about to get in with Riggs when I noticed that Clay hadn't moved. "Yo, Clay! Move your ass."

Clearly lost in his thoughts, he looked up at me and mumbled, "Huh?"

"Move your ass, brother!"

"Oh, shit." He cleared his throat and cocked his head. "Sorry, man. I'm coming!"

As soon as we were both inside, Riggs started up the

engine and pulled out of the parking lot. We hadn't been driving long when I glanced over at Clay and was surprised to see that he still looked a little rattled. I didn't necessarily blame him. I remembered my first run and how nervous I was. I wasn't just worried that the brothers and I would get busted and end up in jail; I was afraid that I might fuck something up and end my chance of becoming a member of Satan's Fury. Hoping to ease Clay's mind, I gave him a quick nudge and said, "I know this is a lot to take in, but just try and keep a level head. Everything will be fine."

"I'm not worried about this, brother. I mean, don't get me wrong, I know how important all this shit is and that we gotta be careful and all that. Hell, I'll do whatever you need me to do, but something else has been bugging me."

"Oh, really? What's that?"

"I've been seeing this...Oh, hell, it don't matter. I'll tell ya about it later." He looked me in the eye and said, "We need to be focused on the run right now."

"You're right. We do," I agreed. "You know how this is supposed to play out, right?"

"Yeah." Clay nodded. "We'll be at the back of some gas station or something. We check our surroundings...make sure the coast is clear. Once we're sure that nothing looks suspicious or whatever, then we start moving the crates from our trailer into the other truck."

"Yeah, that's pretty much it." There was something about the look in his eyes that didn't set well with me, so I told him, "I tell you what, for today, you just listen to me. I'll tell you what to do and when to do it."

"Okay. I can do that."

"Shouldn't take long," I tried to assure him. "Ten to

fifteen minutes at the most, and then we'll be headed back home."

"How long of a drive we got ahead of us?"

"It's about two hours, depending on traffic."

He nodded. "Okay. I got it."

We were riding in the truck with Riggs and T-Bone, and neither of them had much to say on the way to Little Rock, which made the drive seem longer than usual. Our buyer was an older Hispanic guy named Zerafin Guardian. He'd been working with the club for over twenty years, and we'd never had a single issue during our deliveries. They'd always gone off without a hitch, and we assumed that today would be no different. When we pulled up to the old abandoned gas station, Guardian's refrigerator truck was parked around back, and he and two of his guys were standing by, waiting to help us unload. Murphy and Riggs pulled up next to them, and once they were both parked, I leaned over to Clay and said, "Wait for my signal."

Clay nodded, then watched as Murphy got out of his SUV and went over to Guardian. They spoke for a few moments, then Murphy motioned for us to get out and start unloading. I nudged Clay and said, "Let's go."

We both followed the others over to the back end of the trailer. I unlocked the back door, and once I'd unloaded both horses, T-Bone walked inside and unbolted the secret compartments. As soon as he was finished, the guys started to remove the crates one by one and load them into the backend of Guardian's truck. While it was a smaller load, the crates were fucking heavy as hell, and it took some time to get them moved from one truck to the other. T-Bone and I had just loaded the last crate into the back of his truck when I heard Clay growl, "Son of a bitch!"

Curious, I turned to see what had him pissed and found him reaching into his back holster for his weapon. Before I could make sense of what was happening, he had bolted towards the rear of the building. Stunned, I shouted, "What the fuck?"

"I got no fucking idea, brother," T-Bone replied, shaking his head. "But I guess we best be finding out."

We were just about to start going after him when we heard Murphy shout, "We've got company!"

Just as soon as the words came out of his mouth, gunfire exploded around us, forcing me and T-Bone to duck low as we charged towards the rear of the horse trailer. Bullets whipped over our heads as we withdrew our weapons and surveyed our surroundings, trying to quickly locate our assailants. When I spotted something on one of the rooftops, I turned to T-Bone and said, "On your left. Up on the roof!"

"Got it!" He motioned his hand over to the right as he said, "Another one's over there behind the Mercedes."

"I see him."

Just as we both started shooting, Guardian and his boys jumped into his truck and raced out of the parking lot, leaving us to fight off our attackers alone. T-Bone was still firing away when he grumbled, "What a bunch of fucking pussies!"

"They got their shit," I grumbled. "Nothing keeping them here."

"If he had any fucking self-respect, he would've stayed for us."

T-Bone fired another shot, killing the man cowering behind the Mercedes while I took out the guy on the roof.

Random shots were still being fired behind us, but I'd noticed that they were becoming less and less frequent. When T-Bone and I turned and started back towards the others, Murphy asked, "Hey, you two okay?"

"Yeah, we're good," T-Bone answered. "Any idea who these guys were?"

Murphy shook his head. "Got no clue."

"We gotta figure out what the fuck just happened here," Riggs barked.

"Got no way of knowing," Gunner complained. "We don't know if these guys were already hiding out here or if they could've fucking followed us."

T-Bone ran his hand over his bald head as he grumbled, "Hell, for that matter, we don't even know if they were here for us or for fucking Guardian."

"And with no video surveillance, it's going to be hard to find any answers," Riggs complained.

Just when we were thinking all hope was lost, Clay walked up behind us with some thug who looked like he was all kinds of trouble. He was twenty-two or so, and he was wearing a black t-shirt, black jeans, and white tennis shoes. He was tatted up all the way to his throat, and he had on one of those thick gold chains and oversized diamond earrings in both ears. His face was all busted up, and his hands were bound behind his back. Clay had worked him over good and seemed quite proud of himself as he said, "I got one of those motherfuckers."

"Hell, yeah. That's what I'm talking about," T-Bone hailed. "Where'd you get him?"

"Spotted him sneaking around back just before the shooting started," Clay explained. "Pretty sure I've seen him nosing around the clubhouse a couple of times before.

If I had to guess, I'd say he's the one who brought his buddies here today."

"Wait a fucking minute!" The punk just stood there glaring at us with nothing but pure disgust as I barked, "You're telling me, you knew this kid was nosing around the club and you didn't say nothing?"

Clay shrugged. "I was going to this morning, but I figured I should wait until after the run. Didn't figure he'd have the balls to cause any trouble...not with fucking Fury."

Furious, I had to take in a deep breath to keep myself from punching him in the fucking throat. "Clearly, you were fucking wrong!"

"Easy, brother." Murphy placed his hand on my shoulder. "No way he could've known this shit was gonna go down."

"And he might've actually helped us out here." Riggs reached for the collar of the kid's shirt, lowering just enough to expose the ink on his chest, and said, "Looks like our boy is an *Inner Disciple*."

"What the fuck!" T-Bone roared.

Murphy took a step towards the kid and placed his hand around his throat, gripping tightly as he asked, "Why did you and your boys follow us here today?"

When he didn't answer, Murphy tightened his grip and growled, "Did KeShawn send you here to take us out?"

Still nothing.

Frustrated, Murphy released his grip on the kid's throat and slammed his fist into his gut, causing him to gasp for breath. "I asked you a fucking question!"

"I don't give a fuck," the kid spat. "I ain't gonna tell you motherfuckers *shit*."

"Is that right?" Murphy chuckled. "Wait until we get

you back to the clubhouse and you meet Shadow. You'll tell us everything we want to know."

The kid's eyes widened as he asked, "Who the fuck is Shadow?"

"You'll see."

With that, Murphy grabbed him by the elbow and tugged him towards the SUV. We got the horses loaded up and were on the road headed back to Memphis. Every now and then, Clay would glance over in my direction, but I kept my focus trained straight ahead, paying him absolutely no attention. I knew that he was stewing in his thoughts, worried that he'd fucked up beyond repair. He was hoping that I'd give him some sort of sign that things were going to be okay, but I couldn't do that. Yeah, he'd come through for us by getting his hands on the kid, but that didn't change the fact that he'd fucked up. His mistake could've cost one of us our lives, and that wasn't something I took lightly. Hell, none of us did. We were family, through and through, and the thought of losing any one of them because of some kind of oversight was difficult to stomach. It made me realize that Clay still had a great deal to learn. He'd yet to understand the true value of brotherhood. Unfortunately, that wasn't something that I could teach him. Clay would have to experience it for himself. He'd have to see what it felt like to know that someone always had his back, that the brothers were always loyal to one another and to the club, and would take a bullet if it meant keeping a member safe. I hoped for his sake that he figured it all out because there was no greater feeling on the planet.

Darcy

✥

"So, where have you guys been?"

Caleb was at his station, looking all kinds of hot in his tight-fitting, long-sleeve black t-shirt and faded jeans as he worked on a carburetor. He didn't even look up as he answered, "Had club business to tend to."

I'd already asked one of the other guys several days before, and his reaction had made me slightly curious, so I thought I'd see if Caleb would tell me what they'd actually been doing for the past few days. "Oh, really? What kind of club business?"

I was wrong. He didn't say a thing. Instead, all I got was dead air.

"So, it going to be like that, huh?"

"What?"

"You're just gonna up and disappear for three days and not even tell me what was going on?"

"*I already told you.*" Caleb kept his focus on the grimy carburetor in his hand as he shook his head and replied, "We had club business to tend to."

"That doesn't tell me anything." I don't know why it

aggravated me that he wouldn't answer me. Maybe it was the fact that I'd been busting my ass at the garage while they were all off doing God knows what. I rolled my eyes and grumbled under my breath, "What's up with you guys and your secrets about 'club business' anyway? If I didn't know better, I'd think you were trying to hide something."

He gave me a warning look, and I almost laughed. That look alone was enough to keep me pushing, so I crossed my arms and scowled as I leaned against the side of the Chevy pickup. "So, this thing that no one wants to talk about...is it dangerous?"

"Darcy."

"What?" I asked innocently. "I'm not asking you to tell me what you guys were actually doing. I was just asking if it was dangerous."

"Well, don't." His tone grew firm as he said, "In fact, when it comes to club business, don't ask any questions at all."

"What? Why not?"

"For one, you're an outsider. Club business is never discussed with anyone except members. *Period,*" he answered gruffly. "And then there's the fact that you're a woman."

"A woman? What the hell does that have to do with anything?"

"If you were an ol' lady or even dating a brother, then I might explain it to you." He glanced up at me with a blank expression as he said, "Since you're not, this conversation is over."

"Just like that?"

"Yeah. *Just like that.*"

"Fine." I stood there staring at him for several seconds, then remembered all the projects I'd been working on and still needed to complete. "So, what am I supposed to do about the ticket for the Honda?"

"Just put it on Blaze's desk." He turned his attention back to his work as he continued, "He'll get to it when he can."

I tried to rein in my bitchy tone as I asked, "Any idea when he needs the '58 Duo done?"

"He didn't say, but I'll be sure and ask him if he calls to check in."

"I'd appreciate it."

I turned to leave, but stopped when Caleb called out to me, "Darcy?"

"Yeah?"

When I spun around to face him, I could tell by his expression that something was weighing on his mind. After several moments, he finally said, "You need to know that things can get pretty intense around here. There'll be times when we don't come into the garage for days, weeks even. Sometimes the guys will seem like they're walking on top of the world, while at others they'll seem like they're ready to blow. Like it or not, you're never going to have any idea why things are the way they are around here."

I thought about what he'd said for a moment, then replied, "I get it."

"I hope you do," his dark eyes grew intense as he continued, "because the guys hired you because they thought you could handle it."

I took a moment to think about what he'd said, and I suddenly felt guilty for being such an asshole. Caleb didn't owe me any answers. Hell, none of them did. I was simply an employee—nothing more, and I needed to remember that the next time I got my panties in a twist over something stupid. I let out a sigh and said, "You're right, and I *can* handle it. You'll see."

Before he could say anything more, I went back to my paint room and got to work on the 1958 Harley Duo Glide I'd started on that morning. It was Harley's first model with a rear suspension, and their coil-over shocks were a big hit with riders, making this particular motorcycle an instant classic. It was a ride made for comfort with more chrome than parts that actually needed painting, but once I'd painted it all black and added the intricate flame design on the tank, it would be something to behold. I spent the entire day doing my best to focus on it, and nothing else.

Once I was done, I said a quick goodbye to the guys and headed home. When I got to the trailer, I noticed that two new motion-activated lights had been installed on each corner of the house. I might've stopped and asked Frances or Alice about them, but I already knew who was responsible. As soon as I got inside, I took out my phone and messaged Caleb.

Me: Security lights too?

Caleb: Just helping out Thelma and Louise.

Me: I didn't ask you to do that.

Caleb: No, you didn't. You didn't ask for cameras, but those will be installed next.

Me: I already told you. I don't need all this stuff.

Caleb: Good night, Darcy.

Me: Caleb!

When he didn't respond, I hung up my phone and got ready for bed. The following day, I tried to keep my focus strictly on my work, but there were those moments where I'd find myself looking over to Caleb's station to see what he was up to. I told myself that it didn't mean anything, that it was just my curiosity getting the best of me, but as each day passed, I was beginning to have my doubts. I feared that the pull I felt towards him was growing stronger, but I wouldn't let myself think about that. Instead, I pushed it to the back of my mind, refusing to let it keep me from getting my work done. There had still been no sign of Blaze, so I had no idea when things were expected to be done. It was hard not to let myself get frustrated or overwhelmed. I didn't want to disappoint the guys or my customers by not having something done on time, so I'd been busting my ass to finish one project after the next.

It was almost six on a Friday night, and I'd been at it since daylight. I hadn't even stopped to eat lunch. I was just starting to wind things down when Caleb tapped on the paint room door. As he stepped inside, he asked, "Hey, you hungry?"

"Starving. Why?"

"T-Bone and I are about to go grab a burger at the 8-Ball." He was out of his work overalls and back in his t-shirt and jeans, along with his Satan's Fury cut, and he was looking all kinds of good with his day-old scruff. "Thought I'd see if you wanted to join us."

We hadn't spoken much in the past couple of days, so his offer took me by surprise. If I hadn't been so hungry, I might've considered telling him no. "Can you give me a minute to wrap this up?"

"Yeah. We'll meet you out back when you're done."

"Okay. Sounds good."

I rushed to finish the front fender, then once I'd put away all my equipment, I pulled off my painter's suit and gloves. I went over to the sink and did my best to wash up. After I was done, I grabbed my keys and went out to meet T-Bone and Caleb. They were already sitting on their bikes, and a big smile crossed T-Bone's face as soon as he saw me walking in their direction. "Come on, woman. I'm withering away over here."

"I'm coming. I'm coming!"

A big goofy smile crossed T-Bone's face as he snickered. "Yeah, that's what she said."

I shook my head as I got on my bike. "How old are you? Twelve?"

"I'll show you twelve." He grabbed his crotch as he taunted, "Twelve hard inches."

"*T-Bone*," Caleb fussed.

"What?" T-Bone's brows furrowed with dejection as he motioned his hand in my direction. "She said she wanted to be treated like one of the guys."

"That doesn't mean—"

"It's fine, Caleb," I interrupted. "I can handle it, besides...I know as well as you do, the only thing T-Bone has that's twelve inches is that seat he's sitting on."

"Damn, woman. That's fucking cold."

I giggled as I told him, "Only because it's true."

"What are you two waiting for? Let's go eat."

With that, the guys started their engines, and I followed them over to the 8-Ball. Just like the night when Caleb and I had gone there for a beer, the place wasn't very busy, and we had no problem getting a table. I was feeling a little skeptical as I placed my order for a cheeseburger and fries, but T-Bone leaned over and whispered, "Best fucking burger in town. Swear it."

"I'm so hungry right now I'd eat the heel off my boot as long as it wouldn't make me pay for it later."

"I'm not promising that this burger won't hang with you for a couple of hours, but trust me. It'll be worth it," he assured me.

A pretty young waitress with long blonde hair, large breasts, and long legs brought over our drinks. Her eyes roamed over Caleb as she placed his beer in front of him, making it clear that she found him attractive. "Hey, y'all. I'm Crystal. I'll be your waitress tonight."

Biting back the unexpected twinge of jealousy, I gave her a slight smile. "Hey, Crystal."

With her focus still trained on Caleb, Crystal placed her hand on her hip and smiled. "Can I get you anything else?"

"No." Seeming unfazed by her advances, he replied, "This should do it."

"All right, then. I'll be back as soon as your order is up."

When she turned to leave, T-Bone leaned to the side for a better view of her ass as she walked back to the bar. "Damn, brother. That chick is smoking."

"Um-hmm."

"What? Look at the fine ass on that chick. It's all kinds of fine, and she's totally into you, man," T-Bone pushed. "You should hit that, brother."

I felt my stomach twist into a knot as I watched him glance back over at Crystal. I could see the wheels turning in his head, and I found myself holding my breath as I waited for him to respond. After just a brief moment, he turned his attention back to T-Bone. "Nah, I'm good."

"Damn, brother. I give up." Caleb shook his head, then looked over to me. He held my gaze as he reached for his beer, and my eyes dropped to his mouth as he brought the bottle up to his lips. Damn. I needed to get a grip. I turned to T-Bone and was thankful when he asked, "So, how you like working at the garage so far?"

"It's been good." I could've sworn that Caleb was

staring at me, but when I glanced over in his direction, he was studying the label on his bottle of beer. "I've really liked some of the projects I've been working on."

"The job you did on that '58 Duo was something else." He let out a small grunt of air. "Makes me think I might need to get something done to mine."

"Really? What do you have in mind?"

"I don't know. Something simple, understated...but packs a punch." He cocked his eyebrow and smiled. "Something like me."

Caleb chuckled as he told him, "You are anything but understated, brother."

Caleb wasn't wrong. From the moment I'd met T-Bone, I could tell that he was one of those larger-than-life kind of guys, and it had nothing to do with his enormous size. It was all about his boisterous sense of humor, always laughing and cracking jokes, rarely being serious about anything except the club, and it was impossible not to like the guy. I held back my giggle as a soured expression marked his face. "What? I can be simple and understated."

Before Caleb could respond, Crystal returned with our food. Again, her eyes were trained on Caleb as she placed our plates down on the table. Once she'd finished, she arched her back slightly, pronouncing her very large assets right in Rider's face. "Can I get you guys anything else?"

I thought T-bone's eyes would pop out of his head as he stared across the table at her cleavage. His lips curled into a lopsided grin as he replied, "You could get me your phone number, darlin'."

"Oh, well...um," she stammered, clearly surprised by T-Bone's request. I watched as she looked over and studied him for a moment. When I saw that flicker in her eye, I knew her response even before she said the words. "Sure thing, handsome."

She walked closer to where he sat, wrote her name and number on a napkin, and gave him a sexy smile as she offered it to him. "Give me a call sometime."

"Plan on it."

He never took his eyes off her as she turned and headed back to the bar. Caleb glanced over to me and chuckled under his breath as he reached for his burger. "Yep. Definitely not *simple or understated*."

"No." He motioned over to Crystal as he boasted, "But simple and understated wouldn't have gotten me her phone number."

"Probably not," Caleb scoffed. "What do you think of your burger?"

When I realized he was talking to me, I quickly finished the bite I had in my mouth and swallowed. "You guys were right. It's actually really good."

"I told you," T-Bone mumbled through his mouthful of food. "Best fucking burger around."

We continued to banter back and forth as we ate, and I really enjoyed myself. While they were both members of Satan's Fury—an MC known for its tough-as-nails bikers, they were also just two regular guys who liked to let loose and have a good time now and then. It was nice seeing this side of them, and I hoped I would get more of it in the future. As soon as we'd finished eating, T-Bone looked down at his watch and announced, "Damn, we better get back to the clubhouse."

"Yeah, you're right." Caleb stood and placed a couple of twenties on the table. "I'll meet you back there in about an hour. I'm gonna follow her home first."

"What?" I argued. "Haven't we been over this?"

"Yeah, as a matter of fact *we have*."

I could tell by his tone that there was no sense arguing with him. He'd follow me home whether I wanted him to or not. I trailed behind them out the door, and as we got on our bikes, I called out to T-Bone, "Had a great time. See you on Monday!"

"We're having a get together at the clubhouse tomorrow night. You should drop by."

Since I'd never been to an MC gathering, I asked, "What kind of get together?"

"The kind where there's too much food and beer," he chuckled with his response.

"We're celebrating Gunner and August's engagement," Caleb added. "You should come. It'll be fun."

"Okay. I'll try to make it."

T-Bone was the first to pull out of the parking lot with Caleb and me following close behind. Since he knew where I lived, I decided there was no point in trying to be clever and losing Caleb on the way. Instead, I just enjoyed the beautiful night's ride back to my place. It was just dark enough to see the stars, and the air was just cool enough to keep me wide awake. From time to time, I glanced over at my rearview mirror and felt oddly comforted by the fact that Caleb was right behind me. He remained there as I pulled up to my trailer and parked next to my truck. I was expecting him to simply give me a quick wave and head back to the city, but instead, he parked his bike right next to mine. When he started over to me, I took off my helmet and said, "Well, I made it. Safe and sound."

"That you did."

I'd never been one to get nervous around men, but something about the way he was staring at me sent a shiver down my spine. Hoping to lighten the mood, I smiled and said, "You know, instead of coming all the way out here, you could've been following Crystal home tonight if you hadn't let T-Bone snatch her up."

"T-Bone was welcome to have her."

"Why? Was she not your type or something?" I teased.

He remained silent for what seemed like an eternity before he finally said, "Actually, there's another girl I've had on my mind lately."

"Oh, really?" His declaration caught me off guard. I hadn't even considered the fact that he might have a girlfriend. I had no idea why the thought hadn't entered my mind. Caleb was an attractive guy. It only made sense that he would be involved with someone. I didn't want him to notice my disappointment, so I tried to think of something playful to say in return. Unfortunately, all I could muster was, "I had no idea."

"Hey, I better get going." He turned and walked over to his bike. He threw his leg over the seat, and just as he got settled, he looked over to me and asked, "You coming tomorrow night?"

"Maybe. What time does it start?"

"People will start rolling in around eight, but anytime is fine."

"Okay." As he slipped on his helmet, I called out to him, "Oh, wait a minute! I need to talk to you about those cameras!"

Ignoring me, he started his engine and gave a slight wave as he backed out of my drive, leaving me with no choice but to stand there and watch as his taillights disappeared into the darkness.

Rider

Gunner and I were standing in the doorway of Shadow's workroom, watching as he tried questioning him again. It had been days since we'd brought him in. His clothes were soaked in blood, his body and face swollen with bruises, and yet he'd given us little to no information on the Disciples. Shadow had managed to get him to tell us that his birth name was Anthony Bonds, but his gang called him "Little Ravage." He was twenty-two and had been with the Disciples since he was thirteen. That wasn't much to go on, and we needed answers—now. Knowing what was at stake, frustrations were growing high among the brothers, especially with Shadow. As our enforcer, he'd dealt with all kinds of men—big and small, young and old—but it had never taken him this long to break someone.

Anthony was bound with his arms stretched out away from his body in a standing position, and he was barely conscious when Shadow dumped a bucket of cold water over his head. Anthony raised his head with a gasp and groaned, "Fuck!"

"Welcome back," Shadow growled. "You ready to talk?"

Anthony shook his head. "You know I ain't gonna tell you shit."

"I know that's what you keep saying, but I know something you don't." Shadow grabbed him by the throat, forcing him to look at him. "Every man has his breaking point, and sooner or later, I'll get you there."

"Good luck with that." Anthony mustered what was left of his strength and forced himself into a standing position. "It's only a matter of time before they come here looking for me, and when they do, you fuckers are as good as dead."

"Damn. You're dumber than I thought," Shadow scoffed as he released his throat. "Let me lay it out for you in terms you'll understand. Even if you die in here, without telling us a thing, we'll make them think you ratted them out."

He inhaled a quick breath. "Go ahead. You don't know shit."

"We know that KeShawn's trying to build his numbers by tying up with the Red Knights. He's hoping they'll give him the extra manpower he'd need to take us down." Shadow stood in front of Anthony with his arms crossed, talking in a low monotone that would make any man unnerved. "Also know that he thinks he's been trailing one of our brothers by using some fucking tracking device they put on his truck, and he just got in another shipment of automatic rifles delivered out to his place."

"But how—"

"Doesn't matter how we found out any of it. We'll make them think we got the information from you. Once we've convinced them that you're a fucking snitch, we'll dump you on their doorstep."

"You can't do that, man!" Anthony cried with panic.

"Now, you're getting it." Shadow took a menacing step towards him as he sneered, "Talk or don't talk. Either way, you're fucked."

"And if I tell you what you want to know?"

"They'll never know you said a word," Shadow assured him.

I knew in that moment Shadow had him. Anthony didn't want his crew thinking he was a snitch and was willing to be tortured for days on end to keep that from happening. Shadow was smart enough to use that against him. Anthony cleared his throat, then opened the vault. "Slayer wasn't even planning to take on Fury. He just wanted to make that fucking nurse pay for killing Genocide."

"So, this is all because he thinks she had something to do with his death?"

"Yeah. He knew she fucked around, wasted time, and let our boy die, but he thought it was 'cause he was nothing but a street rat or some bullshit like that. It wasn't until he saw your boys watching her that he put two and two together."

A confused look crossed Shadow's face as he asked, "What the fuck are you talking about?"

"Slayer knows you put your girl up to killing Genocide as some kind of message from your club to ours. That's why he sent a message of his own at your drop-off. That hit the other day was just the beginning." My back stiffened as I listened to him say, "He's going after your garage, that diner you guys hang at, and even this here clubhouse. He's looking to find out where some of you live, so he can get to you there. You better get ready, 'cause shit is about to get real around here, man."

Shadow glanced over in our direction, and I knew

exactly what he was thinking. There was no more guessing if we were gonna have to deal with further bullshit from the Disciples. We now had proof that they were planning their attack. It was just a matter of figuring out what we were gonna do about it. Shadow turned his attention back to Anthony. "You got any idea when he's planning on making these hits?"

"If he had it his way, he would've already done it, but he ain't stupid. He knows he's gotta have more than just our crew to take you fuckers down." Anthony glared at Shadow as he told him, "He's already got the Red Angels on board, but he's still working to get more backing from the Dark Angels. They'll come around though 'cause Slayer isn't gonna stop until he gets his fucking way. You can count on that shit."

After Shadow questioned him for a few more minutes, Gunner and I followed him down to Gus's office to let him know what had transpired. When we walked in, he was sitting at his desk talking with our VP, Moose, and Blaze. Shadow stepped forward and said, "The kid finally cracked."

"And?"

"Looks like we're about to have one hell of a war on our hands."

He spent the next few minutes telling them everything that Anthony had told us. As soon as he was done, Moose shook his head. "Damn, Lewis has always been a loose cannon, but fuck, I never thought he'd take things this far."

"Losing a kid is hard. Knowing he's responsible can break him. Lewis is looking to shift the blame so he doesn't have to admit the truth." Gus ran his hand over his beard and grumbled something incoherently under his breath. "We need to end this thing before it gets any more out of hand."

"Don't disagree with you there," Blaze growled. "I say we take the fucker and his gang down tonight. End every last one of them."

I wasn't surprised by Blaze's reaction. After all, it was his ol' lady who was under the highest threat. Gus was fully aware of how he felt when he told him, "We're going to handle this, brother, but we're not going in with blinders on. We gotta know what we're facing."

"Gus is right. If Lewis is trying to build his numbers, then we need to find out for sure if the Red Knights have joined up with him and who else is considering it," Moose added.

"I'll make some calls and see what I can find out. It'll take some time, but if he's gained new allies, my contacts will know about it." Gus turned to Blaze as he asked, "Any word from Riggs on the cameras?"

"Yeah. He and Gauge managed to get them up, but they're having some issues with the feed," Blaze explained. "He's hoping to have it all operating by the end of the night."

"Good. We'll meet back first thing in the morning and start making preparations." Gus stood up from his desk with a determined look in his eye. "Lewis might be too blind to see it, but the Disciples' days are numbered."

"Hell yeah, they are," Blaze roared.

"I'll see you boys in the morning. Church at six."

With that, we all started to walk out of Gus's office. We were almost through the door when Gunner suddenly stopped and asked, "What about tomorrow night?"

Until then, I'd all but forgotten about his and August's

engagement celebration. Since August was Gus's daughter, we knew it was an important night, especially for Gus. He'd only recently found out that he had a daughter, and having August and his granddaughter, Harper, in his life now meant a great deal to him. Knowing he wouldn't want to put either of them in danger, I assumed he would cancel the party, but to my surprise, he replied, "As for now, it's still on. We'll double security and monitor Lewis's every move. If it looks like we're going to have trouble, we'll call a lock down."

"Understood."

It was already late when we left Gus's office, so I decided to skip going home and just crashed at the club-house. I was glad I did. We hit the ground running at five-thirty the following morning. I'd barely had a chance to down a cup of coffee before it was time to meet for church. As soon as we were all gathered in the conference room, we picked apart every bit of information we'd collected on the Disciples and started formulating the best plan for taking them down. The Disciples would soon regret the moment they decided to go up against Satan's Fury.

Before we were dismissed, Gus gave out assignments for each of us to complete before the gathering. T-Bone and I were to help Murphy check all the artillery, not only to make sure we had everything we needed, but that it also was in working order. I followed them both over to the clubhouse storage room. There wasn't much to it. Just a medium-sized room with two large metal tables in the center and safes lining the back wall. As soon as we walked in, Murphy started unlocking the safes while T-Bone and I unloaded all the guns and ammo. T-Bone grabbed an armful, and as he headed out the back, he grumbled,

"Wish I had me a couple of those Disciple fuckers I could use for target practice."

"You and me both." I watched as he loaded his first AR and shot off a few rounds. There was something about his expression that had me asking, "You all right?"

"Yeah. Just ready to get this shit done" He glanced over at me with a smirk. "Crystal is coming to the party tonight."

"Damn. I'm impressed you actually convinced her to go out with you," I poked.

"Wasn't any convincing to be done." He grabbed another rifle and shot off several rounds. "She knew a good thing when she saw it."

I picked up one of the Glocks and fired a few test shots, then moved on to the next. With Murphy on one side of me and T-Bone on the other, the three of us continued to test each and every weapon. After we were done, we went back to the storage room and spread out all the ammo, then filled all the different magazines and took inventory of what was remaining. We were just starting to wrap things up when Murphy turned to me and said, "I thought we'd run over to KeShawn's place and check things out when we finish up here."

"Sounds good."

Concerned, T-Bone asked, "You sure it's a good idea for them to see you there?"

"For tonight, we'll lay low. Don't want to stir up any trouble before the party." Murphy closed his case of ammo and moved to the next. "But if something's going on over there, I want us to be the first to know about it."

"You've got a good point." T-Bone motioned his hand for us to leave. "You two go ahead. I'll finish this up."

"You sure?"

"Absolutely."

Murphy and I drove over to KeShawn's place. Unlike the times before, we tried our best not to draw attention to ourselves and parked in seclusion. We sat there until almost dark, but unfortunately, there wasn't much to see. Most of their crew were pretty quiet, so Murphy looked over to me and said, "Nothing's happening here. Let's head back to the clubhouse."

"You got it."

By the time we made it back, most of the guys were already there and setting up the bonfire. Murphy headed home to pick up Riley while I went inside to take a shower. When I was done, I went back out to join the others at the bonfire. I was having a good time with my brothers, drinking a beer and shooting the shit, but every time I saw a set of headlights pull through the gate, I'd find myself checking to see if it was Darcy. For over an hour, it was one disappointment after the next, but just as I was giving up hope, I spotted her bright red pickup.

I grabbed us both a beer from the cooler, then headed over to the edge of the parking lot to wait for her. Once she was parked, she fumbled around inside for several moments, then finally opened the door and stepped out. As soon as her high heels hit the ground, I knew I was in trouble. My eyes followed the line of her long, slender legs up to the hem of her black mini-skirt, which had inched its way up her thigh during her drive over. Damn. She looked down and slightly shimmied her hips, adjusting her skirt as she took a quick look around the parking lot. I watched as her beautiful, pouty lips slowly curved into a sexy smile the second she spotted me. Fuck. I'd never seen a more beautiful sight.

She closed the door to her truck, and I couldn't take

my eyes off her as she started towards me. That little black skirt hugged her curves in all the right places, bringing my cock to life right there in the fucking parking lot. At that moment, all my thoughts of the Inner Disciples were instantly forgotten. When she made it over to me, she smiled and said, "Hey, how's it going?"

"It's going good." I motioned over to the bonfire. "The guys and I were starting to wonder if you were going to make it."

"I almost didn't, but some friends of mine convinced me to come."

"Thelma and Louise?"

She giggled with a nod. "Yeah. They can be pretty persistent when they put their minds to it."

"I bet they can." As I offered her a beer, I asked, "You want to join the others at the fire or go inside to the bar?"

"Fire's good."

I nodded, then turned and started towards the others. As soon as the guys noticed Darcy walking in their direction, several of them called, "Darcy! Glad you made it."

"Thanks for the invite."

"Kind of strange seeing you out of your painter's suit." T-Bone took a step back and gave her the once over. "You clean up pretty good."

"I wish I could say the same for you," she teased.

They all started laughing, and a slew of bad one-liners ensued as each of them tried to one-up the other. As I stood there next to her, watching her hold her own with my brothers, it was hard to resist slipping my arm around her waist and claiming her as mine as we stood there with the others. When Darcy finished her beer, I took the empty bottle from her hand and asked, "You want another one?"

"Yeah, sure."

"I'll be right back."

I walked over and grabbed us both a cold one out of the cooler. When I turned to head back, I found Darcy standing next to me. She took one of the bottles out of my hand and smiled. "Thanks."

"No problem." She didn't seem eager to get back to the others though. "Are you having a good time?"

"I am, but I could use a minute to catch my breath."

"I can understand that. The guys can get carried away sometimes."

"They're great." I could tell by the sound of her voice that she meant it. "I've really enjoyed getting to know them."

"I'm pretty sure they feel the same way about you."

"I hope so." After several moments, she crossed her arms and said, "So, um...tell me about this girl who's caught your fancy."

"Caught my fancy?"

"You know—the girl you were telling me about last night. The one you're interested in."

"What do you want to know?"

"Everything."

As soon as the words came out of her mouth, her posture changed. Her back stiffened as she shoved her hands in the back pocket of her skirt, and the muscles in her neck tightened. It was almost like she was trying to brace herself for what I was about to say, making me wonder if I should redirect the conversation. "What is it with women and all their questions?"

"Come on, Caleb. Don't go trying to avoid the question." She pulled her long auburn hair to the side, letting it cascade down her shoulder as she looked up at me with those beautiful blue eyes. "Just tell me what she's like."

"Well, she's beautiful and smart...talented like you wouldn't believe."

Raking her teeth over her bottom lip, she pushed, "Um-hmm. What else?"

"She's also infuriating as hell." I chuckled under my breath as I watched her brows furrow. "Yeah, she's about as stubborn as they come—short-tempered and hard to predict. One minute she's sweet as honey, and the next, she's likely to rip your balls right off...and for the life of me, I just can't get her out of my head."

"Wow." Sounding almost disappointed, Darcy muttered, "She sounds like she's really something."

I took a step towards her, closing the gap between us, and her eyes widened with surprise as I rested my hands on her hips. "You're right...*You are.*"

"What?" she gasped. "You were talking about *me?*"

Confusion marked her face as she tried to make sense of what I'd said. She was still trying to work it out in her head when I replied, "Yes, Darcy. *You.*"

I leaned forward with my mouth hovering over hers for what seemed like a lifetime, waiting for some sign that I was making the wrong move. When she didn't resist or even show the slightest hesitation, I took my chance. I lowered my mouth to hers and kissed her, long and hard. I hadn't wanted to let myself admit it, but it was a kiss I'd been waiting for as long as I could remember. I felt her body trembled as I delved further into her mouth, exploring every inch with my tongue. A light moan of need escaped from her throat as we both inched closer. Damn. I'd tried to fight it, but the pull I felt towards her was even stronger than I thought. I wanted Darcy Harrington, every fucking inch of her, and if this kiss was any indication, she felt the same way about me. The kiss was quickly becoming heated when she placed her hands on my chest, gently pushing me off her. "I'm gonna need a minute here."

I didn't say a word. Instead, I gave her the time she asked for.

After several moments, her breath started to steady and a spark of annoyance flashed through her eyes. "You think I'm infuriating as hell?"

"You have your moments."

"Well, I have news for you, Caleb Hughes...*you*"—she cocked her eyebrow high—"can be pretty damn infuriating yourself."

"Oh, really?" Amused, I crossed my arms and grinned. "And how's that?"

"You're bossy and pig-headed, especially when it comes to something you want."

"Can't disagree with you there."

"You're also..."

Before she could finish her sentence, Riggs came around the back of the clubhouse and called out to me. "Hey, Rider!"

"Yeah?"

"Need you for a minute."

"Be right there." When I turned back to Darcy, she was looking up at me with a frustrated expression, making it clear that she still had things she wanted to say. I wanted to hear every fucking word, but now wasn't an option. Even in situations like these, the club came first.

Darcy

❦

"I need to go see what that is about."

As much as I wanted to finish what he'd started, I simply nodded. "Okay."

"I shouldn't be long."

"I'll be fine, Caleb."

"At least let me take you into the bar." He motioned his head towards the back door of the clubhouse. "You can hang out with the other ol' ladies until I get done."

While I'd met most of the brothers at some point at the garage, I hadn't met any of their women, and the thought of sitting in a room full of people I didn't know made me feel a little uneasy. "I'll just hang out here until you're done."

"Not leaving you out here alone, Darcy."

"Okay, fine. I'll wait in the bar for you."

I followed him inside the clubhouse bar, and I was surprised by how big the place was. There was a large counter at the front with barstools all the way around, and seven or eight tables in the back. They had a jukebox in one corner, several pool tables and dart boards, and a large seating area with a sofa and a couple of chairs in the other. As soon as we started walking towards the front, several of the women turned, glancing over their shoulders as they watched us make our way over to them. A feeling of dread washed over me when I noticed two of them whispering back and forth, making me wish I'd never agreed to come inside. Caleb led me over to one of the empty stools next to the chick with long brown hair and eyes that were so dark they almost looked black. As I sat down next to her, she smiled and said, "You must be Darcy!"

"I am."

"Well, it's good to finally meet you." A smile spread across her face as she placed her hand on mine. "Blaze has been talking nonstop about the work you've been doing in the garage."

"Has he?"

"Girl, yes. The man is crazy about that garage, and he's really glad that you agreed to come work there. He said orders for paint work have doubled since you started working there." She glanced up at Caleb and said, "Don't you have somewhere you need to be?"

"Yeah, I do."

"Well, get going. We've got her," she assured him.

When he glanced down at me, I nodded. "I'll be fine."

"I'll be back." When he started to walk towards the exit, he looked back over to the other women and warned, "You girls behave."

"Hush. You know we will," one of the others teased.

As soon as he walked out, all eyes turned to me. They each took a moment to introduce themselves, not only by name but also whose ol' lady they were. I had to admit that after the third introduction the names started to jumble together. It wasn't all my fault.

I was still reeling from my conversation with Caleb and the kiss we shared, and then I was suddenly thrown into a group of women I'd never laid eyes on before. It was a lot to take in. Once they were all done, I smiled and told them all, "It's really great to finally meet y'all. I've heard the guys talk about each of you at the garage, and now I can finally put a face with your names."

"The guys talk about you too." A big smile spread across Kenadee's face when she said, "They say you're very talented."

"That's very sweet of them. I've been trying really hard to do my best."

"From the sounds of it, you've done great." She gave me a little nudge as she chuckled. "And you made quite an impression your first day."

"Oh, really?" I couldn't remember what she was talking about, so I asked, "Why's that?"

"That whole thing with T-Bone." She giggled as she shook her head. "I would've loved to have been a fly on the wall for that."

"Oh, yeah. Now that I've gotten to know him a little better, I kinda feel bad for crawling him like I did."

"Girl, don't sweat that for a minute." Alex leaned forward. "It was the best thing you could've done. It's the first time the guys have had a woman around their business, and it was a lesson for all of them."

Riley nodded. "She's right."

"Well, I've really enjoyed working with them. They've got a really good thing going down at the garage. People all over talk about the work they do." I took a quick glance around and noticed that most of the guys were gone—only three or four I'd never even seen before remained behind. After I finished off the last of my beer, I asked her, "Where did they all go anyway?"

A pained expression marked Kenadee's face as she slightly shrugged. "There's a situation that they're trying to deal with before it gets out of control."

"You seem concerned about it."

"I am." The others fell silent, letting me know she wasn't the only one who was worried. "We all are, but the guys will handle things. They always do."

Before I could reply, Riley changed the subject. "She's right. They'll take care of it. There doesn't seem to be anything these men can't do...except put their socks in the laundry basket."

"Girl, don't I know it!" Reece groaned as she took a sip of her drink. "They can't seem to put a dirty dish in the sink either."

"Well .." Alex started with a mischievous smirk on her face.

"Well, *what?*" Reece pushed.

"Okay, so...the other night, I walked into the kitchen."

"And?"

"And Shadow was in there...washing dishes." A pale pink blush crept up her neck. "I don't know about you, but there is something *all kinds of sexy* about a man who will help out in the kitchen. Damn, I can't remember the last time I was that turned on."

"I've gotta favor to ask." Kenadee giggled as she asked, "Will you tell that story in front of Blaze?"

"She needs to tell that story in front of *all* the guys," Riley snickered.

We'd just gotten another round of drinks, which included a beer and a shot, when another young brunette walked into the bar. As soon as Kenadee noticed, she waved her over. "Hey, August! Come here and take a load off."

She seemed a little frazzled when she reached us and sat down next to me. "I finally got Harper down."

"Is your mother watching her?"

August nodded. "Just until Gus gets ready to leave. Then, they're taking her over to his place for the night."

"Good." Kenadee looked over to me as she said, "Have you had a chance to meet Darcy yet? She's the one the guys hired to work out at the garage."

"The painter?"

"Yeah, that would be me. It's nice to meet you, August."

Alex leaned over to me and said, "August is Gunner's ol' lady and Gus's daughter."

"Gus? As in *the-president-of-the-club*, Gus?"

"The one and only. They just recently found out about one another, so it's been an adjustment for both of them."

"Oh, wow. That must've been quite a shock."

"Yeah, you could say that again," August scoffed.

"Hey, I've been meaning to ask," Reece interrupted. "Are we still going to meet up for breakfast at the diner tomorrow?"

"I don't know." Doubt crossed Alex's face. "I've really been looking forward to it, but Shadow was pretty adamant that we postpone."

"Blaze was too," Kenadee replied in almost a pout.

"Why? It's not like they don't have eyes on us all the time." Reece nodded her head to the guys behind us and sighed. "And it's not like we're going far—it's just the diner."

"They just want us to be safe."

"Sometimes they go a little overboard." Kenadee

turned to August and me as she said, "We don't get a chance to get together that often unless there's a party or a lockdown, so we decided to starting meeting once a month for breakfast."

"That's cool."

"It's usually a lot of fun. It's just that we have some things going on right now, so it's probably better for us to just do what the guys want and postpone."

"You two should come join us the next time," Kenadee suggested. "We usually try to get to Daisy Mae's by ten."

"I'd like that."

"Give me your number, and I'll text you the next time we decide to get together."

Just as Kenadee finished keying my number into her cell, the guys started coming back into the bar. I grabbed another beer and watched as they each went over to their women and made sure that all was well. I took a quick glance around, but found no sign of Rider or Gunner. I was about to ask Kenadee where they might be, but quickly noticed that she and Alex were busy talking to Shadow and Blaze. Some of the others had gone to play a round of pool, leaving August and me alone. Deciding to strike up a conversation, I turned to her and asked, "So, how do you like being the president's daughter?"

"I don't really know just yet." An odd expression crossed her face. "Like Kenadee said, I just found out that he's my father, so I'm still learning how all this club stuff works."

I was suddenly starting to feel the effects of the beer and shots. "So, you've never been around an MC before?"

"God, no. I hadn't even been around a motorcycle until the day Gus took me for my first ride," she scoffed.

"You don't ride?"

"No. Just with Gunner...and that one time with Gus." She motioned her hand, letting the girl behind the bar know she wanted a beer. "Growing up, my folks just weren't into that sort of thing, so I never really got the opportunity."

"And now that things have changed?"

With narrowed eyes, she eased back in her seat and looked at me like I had three heads. "Would I want to have my own bike?"

"Yeah, your own bike. Your own cut. The whole nine yards."

"I never really thought about it."

Just as she replied, Rider walked over to us with Gunner and an older gentleman with a long, thick beard and dark, piercing eyes. I'd heard the stories about him and knew right away that he was Gus—the famous president of Satan's Fury. I might've been unnerved by the fact, but I was feeling just a tad tipsy.

Gunner slipped his arm around August as he asked, "You girls having a good time?"

"We are. How about you?" I could hear the concern in her voice as she asked, "Is everything okay?"

"Everything's fine." Gunner looked over to Gus, then asked, "Have you had a chance to meet Darcy yet?"

"No, can't say that I have." He extended his hand towards me with a small smile. "Been hearing lots of good things about you."

"You have?"

"Blaze has been very pleased about the work you've been doing over there." He ran his hand over his thick beard as he studied me for a moment. "Also heard you put T-Bone in his place."

"Apparently you aren't the only one who's heard about

that." I could feel Caleb standing next to me, watching me intently as I spoke, "T-Bone and I are straight now."

"Heard that too."

August leaned towards Gunner and Gus as she looked up with a playful smirk. "Darcy and I have been talking and...she thinks I should get a motorcycle of *my own*."

I'd heard the stories about Gus and knew he was a man you didn't go up against. He was known to lead with an iron fist, never taking shit off of anyone, and from the looks of him, I had no doubt that the stories about him were true. It was clear from his expression that he wasn't pleased that I'd suggested that his daughter get a bike of her own. "Is that right?"

"Now, hold up a minute." I suddenly regretted my entire conversation with August. I'd let the haze of the alcohol I'd consumed cloud my thinking. I tried to set things straight, but only ended up making matters worse when I told him, "I was just asking if she'd ever thought about getting one of her own, but I don't see what harm it could do for her to have one...Unless you have something against your woman having her own motorcycle."

Gus's voice was deep and raspy, commanding complete attention as he spoke. "From what I hear, you not only ride, but you have a bike of your own."

"Yeah. I do."

"Okay, then." A smile crossed his face as he said, "There you go. We do have women that not only ride, but own a bike of their own."

"Wait," I argued. "I don't count. I'm just an employee."

"You're tied to Satan's Fury just the same."

His answer came as a surprise to me. I thought I was just working for them. I didn't realize that they considered me tied to them. I was both flattered and terrified by the thought. I was still trying to wrap my head around his last statement. I hadn't noticed that Caleb inched closer until I'd glanced up at him. I could tell by his expression that he was worried about what I might say next. Sadly, that didn't stop me from saying, "Tied to Fury or not, I'm still just an employee. What I'm riding or not riding doesn't really matter. Now, with your ol' ladies, that's something different all together. Makes me wonder...You've got a thing for having your women behind you instead of beside you?"

I'd barely gotten the words out of my mouth when Caleb cleared his throat with a loud grumble, then further interrupted me by saying, "I don't know about y'all, but I could use another beer. *Maybe two.*"

"Yeah, I could definitely go for one," Gunner replied. "August too."

"You got it." He took me by the hand and gave me a gentle tug, leading me out of my seat. "Darcy and I will round us up a few cold ones."

"But...I don't," I started to argue, but stopped as Caleb led me through the crowd. When I realized we weren't going to get the others another beer, I looked back over at Gus and Gunner and found them both smiling from ear to ear. It was clear that they were quite amused by Caleb's little stunt, but I, on the other hand, was not.

Rider

Once I had Darcy in my room, I slammed the door behind us and turned to face her. With a flushed pink face and gorgeous blue eyes blazed, she threw her arms up in the air. "What the hell was that, Caleb? I wasn't done with my conversation!"

"Oh, no. You're wrong about that." I could still remember how hard-headed Darcy could be when we were kids. The minute she'd set her mind to something, I knew there'd be no changing it, so I'd just end up letting it go. This was different. This time, we weren't just a couple of kids arguing over trivial shit. This time, she'd crossed a line, and I wasn't going to simply let it go. "That conversation was done the minute you started talking about women and the club."

"And why would that be?"

"Because you don't have a clue about what goes on here or how things work," I barked.

She propped her hands on her hips defiantly, "But I was making a good point before you yanked me out of there!"

"You do *not* question the president of Satan's Fury about who he gets to fucking prospect! Hell, you don't question him about anything!"

"Pfft. Well, that's just stupid. I was just—"

"*Darcy.*"

"Damn. You've got your panties in all kinds of a twist." She rolled her eyes indignantly as she huffed, "I simply asked the man if—"

"Damn," he grumbled, cutting me off yet again. "You're even more bull-headed than I remember."

Her eyes narrowed as she took a charging step towards me. "Why? Because I asked the man a question?"

"No. Because you're wrong."

"Fine. I'll admit that, all things considered, it might not have been the best topic of conversation, but I wouldn't go so far as to say that I was *wrong.*"

"That's because you're so fucking stubborn." I ran my hand through my hair in aggravation. "The brothers here treat their women with nothing but respect. There's nothing in the world they wouldn't do for them. They'd lay down their lives in order to protect them, and their women know it. They never have to question their loyalty or love towards them. Never. So, just to make sure I'm being perfectly clear—where the ol' ladies ride has nothing to do with whether or not the guys want them at their side. It's simply where the women want to be."

"You're right. I clearly didn't realize what I was saying, and I should've kept my mouth shut. I'm sorry." Darcy cocked her eyebrow as she added, "But just to make sure I'm being perfectly clear, I am *not* stubborn!"

This woman was going to drive me to the point of insanity. Darcy had a stubborn streak a mile long, but damn if I didn't find her sexy as hell when she dug her heels in. I could see her winding herself up to come at me again, and I just couldn't hold back anymore. I ran my hand behind her neck and pulled her parted lips to mine, silencing her with a kiss.

As soon as her tender, full mouth pressed against mine, her tense muscles melted into my arms. Darcy wound her arms around my neck, and as she kissed me back, I found myself thinking back to all those fantasies I'd had about her in high school. I was just a teenager, but even then, I knew how incredible she would feel in my arms. I was consumed by her, then and now, and there wasn't a damn thing I could do about it. She pulled back from our embrace just long enough to whisper my name, "Caleb."

I looked down at her, and when our eyes met, I said, "Tell me."

She didn't answer.

Instead, she remained silent and stared at me with lust-filled eyes, making me want her even more. I wound my fist in her hair and pulled her back to my mouth. She let out a needful moan when the once tender kiss quickly changed, becoming more intense and heated. She opened wider, inviting me to claim her with my mouth. Damn. Darcy felt so fucking good in my arms, and as my hands drifted to her hips, pulling her closer, I wondered where else I'd like to claim her body. Just thinking about tasting and exploring every inch of her naked body was making me grow harder by the second. When she looked up at me, I could not only see, but I could also feel the need radiating off of her. As much as I wanted to take her right then and there, I wasn't going to push. She would have to say the words.

We continued to kiss, and as I held her close to my chest, the moment I waited for finally happened. She shifted her hips, grinding against my growing erection as her heated moan shuddered through her chest. I gave her hair a gentle tug, then lowered my mouth to her ear and whispered, "Tell me what you want, Darcy."

"You *know* what I want."

"I want to hear the words." Darcy studied me for a moment, and fearing she might not follow through, I demanded, "Tell me."

Her eyes met mine as she placed the palm of her hand on my cheek. "I want you, Caleb."

As soon as the words came out of Darcy's mouth, I was done. I kissed her once more, long and hard, then pulled my t-shirt over my head. I watched as her hungry eyes dropped to my chest. While gnawing her bottom lip, she ran her fingertips over my muscles and trailed them along my ink and down my abdomen. She reached my waist and made quick work of my belt and fly, then started to tug at my jeans.

I stepped out of my boots, then pulled off my socks, jeans, and boxers. Leaning down, I lifted her into my arms and cradled her against my bare chest as I carried her over to my bed. Carefully, I lowered her onto the mattress, then slipped off her heels. Darcy lay perfectly still as my hands reached for the hem of her mini-skirt, slowly easing it, along with her white lace thong, down her long, lean legs. With every inch of exposed skin, I could feel the blood surge to my cock. I took my time, using every bit of resistance to rein in my hunger for her so I could save it all for the moment I slid deep inside her. Darcy's eyes never left mine as I pulled off her top and ran my fingers along the lace cup of her bra. I shifted the soft fabric to the side as I took her nipple firmly in my mouth. She arched her back towards me as I swirled my tongue around her sensitive flesh that begged for more. Damn. She felt so good, tasted so good that it was nearly impossible to keep myself from completely losing it. Needing more, I trailed my mouth down past her navel, and her moans filled the room as I kissed and nipped at her soft, delicate skin.

I centered myself between her legs, spreading them wide as I raked my tongue firmly across her clit. Her fingers wound into the sheets, twisting them in her hands, as I continued to tease her with my mouth. I never took my eyes off of hers as I relentlessly licked and sucked, back and forth, relishing the way her body reacted to my every touch. Darcy was close, and after just a few more moments, her body grew rigid with her release. Seeing that satisfied look on her face made it impossible to wait a moment longer. I had to be inside her.

I reached into the drawer beside the bed for a condom, and as I began to rip it open, she took it from my hand. "Wait…it's my turn to play."

A mischievous look crossed her face as she bit her lip and slowly positioned herself at my hips. Her greedy eyes fixed on my throbbing cock as her fingers wrapped around me. The moment her tongue swirled around the head, I was lost. Hell, a fucking train could have come through that room and I wouldn't have noticed.

"Damn, woman," I groaned. "I like the way you play."

Her lips curled into a smile as she started slowly moving her hand up and down my hard shaft, gradually tightening her fingers around me. Her mouth felt so fucking good around my cock. My hands dropped to her head, tangling in her long auburn hair, as she opened her mouth wider, taking me deep. When I felt myself press against the back of her throat, a hiss slipped through my teeth, and before I could rebound, she quickened her pace, nearly sending me over the edge. Her warm, wet mouth was driving me wild, but I wanted more.

I slipped my hands under her arms, pulled her forward and then quickly rolled us over, and as I looked down at her beautiful yet confused face, I growled, "Your mouth is incredible, but I need to be inside you. *Now.*"

After grabbing the condom from the bed, I slipped it on and centered myself at her entrance. Her eyes instantly locked on mine. They were wild and fiery, her desire evident. She wrapped her legs invitingly around my waist, pulling me closer and grinding her center against my hard cock. I couldn't wait anymore.

"Yes," she moaned as I slid deep inside her. I felt her breath tremble, and I paused, reveling in the warm, wet heat of her pussy. It was so tight and perfect that I had to fight the urge to come just from being inside her.

"Fuck, you feel so damn good," I growled and started to move, thrusting harder and deeper with every drive, building up to a relentless pace. Each was more demanding than the last, and I could feel Darcy pulsing around me as her orgasm began to take hold. She shifted her hips forward in the same heated rhythm, giving as good as she got.

"Oh, God! Caleb, don't stop! Yes!"

"Fuck," I groaned. Her body jolted beneath me and she clenched my rock-hard cock, milking me as I continued to drive into her. The sounds of our bodies pounding against one another and echoing around the room made me want to claim her in the most carnal way. At that moment, I slipped my hands under her hips and lifted her, grinding the tips of my fingers into her ass as I buried myself even farther. A deep, tortured growl raked through me as I came inside her. I stilled, relishing in the sensation. After a few moments I removed the condom and tossed it into the trash, then lowered myself down onto the bed beside her. When she rolled to her side, I put my arm around her while she rested her head on my shoulder.

We lay there in silence, listening to the sounds of our ragged breaths start to slow. I was still trying to gather my senses when Darcy propped up on her elbow and glared at me. "Just so you know, I am not stubborn. I'm...strong-willed."

"That's the first thing that comes to your mind after we just..." I shook my head and chuckled. "Really?"

"Well, I'm just..."

"No, Darcy. That in itself goes to show just how damn stubborn you really are." I cocked my eyebrow at her as I said, "But I'm not complaining. Hell, as fucked up as it is, I actually like that you're 'strong-willed,' as you call it."

"I'm not the only one, you know." A smirk crossed her face. "You're pretty damn stubborn yourself."

"Oh, you think so?"

"Um-hmm." She nodded. "Sure do. Otherwise, I wouldn't have two new security lights on my trailer."

"That's not being stubborn. That's being smart." I leaned forward and pressed my lips against her shoulder. "You've got to be careful when you live alone like you do, even with Thelma and her sidekick, Louise."

"I've done just fine, thank you very much."

"Not disagreeing with you. Just stating a fact." When she started to slip on her panties, I sat up and asked, "What are you doing?"

"I'm going home."

"It's late, and you've been drinking." She was just about

to put on her shirt when I reached for her, gently pulling her back to the bed. "Stay here tonight."

"I would, but I can't." She slipped it over her head then added, "I've got things I need to do tomorrow."

"Like what?"

"Things."

"So, these things you have to do...Are they urgent?"

"No, not exactly."

I wrapped my arm around her waist and pulled her against me. "Then, there's no reason for you to rush off."

"*Caleb.*"

"Are you really going to give me a hard time about this, too?"

A soft smile crossed her face as she nestled into the crook of my arm. "No, I guess not. I've got a change of clothes in my truck, so I guess I could just get ready here in the morning."

"See? Giving in wasn't so hard, now was it?"

"No, but don't get used to it."

"I wouldn't dare."

I pulled the covers over us, and it wasn't long before we both drifted off to sleep. The next morning, we were both sleeping soundly when there was a knock at my door. Being careful not to wake Darcy, I eased out of bed and pulled on my boxer briefs. When I opened the door, I found Shadow standing there with a concerned expression. "We're meeting for church in fifteen."

"Is something up?"

"We're making a move. Gus will explain everything when we meet."

"Okay. I'll be there."

I closed the door, and when I turned around, I found

Darcy sitting up on the bed, staring at me. "Is everything okay?"

"It will be." I walked over to my dresser and grabbed a fresh t-shirt and a pair of jeans. As I started getting dressed, I told her, "Going to need you to be careful today if you head over to the diner."

"Umm...okay?"

"And I'm going to get one of the prospects to follow you over there."

She rolled her eyes. "That's not necessary."

"Maybe not. Doing it just the same." I leaned forward and pressed my lips against hers. "I'll call when I can."

"Okay."

When I turned and headed for the door, I couldn't help but notice the strange expression that marked Darcy's face. It was clear that she was concerned about something. Even though I needed to get to church, I stopped and asked, "You got something on your mind?"

"I was just wondering about last night." Her teeth raked across her bottom lip as she studied me for a moment. "What exactly was that?"

"Not sure what you're getting at."

A sigh slipped through her lips as she muttered, "Never mind. It's nothing."

"You talking about what happened between us?" She looked up, and when her eyes met mine, she nodded. "Then, it's definitely *not nothing*."

"Oh."

"We've got something here. Hell, we proved that last night." I walked back over to her and kissed her once more. "Plan on proving it again real soon."

With great reluctance, I forced myself to leave the room

and started towards the conference room. As much as I hated to leave Darcy, especially when she was having doubts about us, I didn't have a choice. My brothers needed me. When I walked in, most of them were already there and had claimed their place at the table. Like me, each of them knew why we'd been called to church and were eager to hear the plan of attack against the Inner Disciples. The room fell silent when Gus approached the table. "I just got a call from Tyrone Davis. As you all know, he and his brother are in charge of the Dark Angels. He told me how Lewis has been trying to recruit them to team up with his crew to take us down."

"Why would he do that?" Moose asked with surprise.

"Seems he and his brother have had some issues with Lewis, and they want him gone...for good. So much so, they're willing to help us out."

Blaze leaned forward as he asked, "Help us out *how?*"

"He and his crew want to join up with us. Get rid of him before he winds up with more than the Red Knights on his side. I normally wouldn't consider rushing into something like this, but I think he's right. Lewis is a problem who needs to be dealt with immediately."

"And how are we going to do that?" Gunner asked.

"Tyrone got word that Lewis has called a meet at Momma D's at seven," Gus answered. "We hit there and his place, and wipe him out once and for all."

As usual, T-Bone was the only one willing to ask the one question that was weighing on all of our minds. "You sure this Tyrone guy is someone we can trust?"

"No way to know for certain. That's why we aren't using his help." Gus ran his hand down his beard as he turned to Murphy. "We good on ammo?"

"More than good."

Gus turned to Blaze as he asked, "You check with Mack and make sure the med packs are ready?"

"Yeah, we're good."

"Riggs, what's the word on the security cameras at Lewis's place?"

"They're up and rolling," Riggs answered. "I've been keeping an eye on him all night."

"Good. I want to know every move this sonofabitch makes."

"You got it."

Gus's voice was low and threatening as he looked out at us and said, "Tonight, Lewis and everyone tied to him goes down."

"Good riddance, motherfucker," Blaze grumbled.

"I want everything prepped and ready to roll before dark," Gus ordered.

"Understood," we all replied.

As soon as he gave the word, the brothers all stood and started to disperse. Gunner and I were just about to walk out of the room when Blaze came up behind us. "Have you two heard anything from the girls?"

"No. Not since church started," Gunner answered.

Concern crossed Blaze's face as he said, "I've been trying to reach Kenadee, but she hasn't answered."

"What about Gauge?" Gunner asked.

"Nothing. Same with Rip and Dane."

"Don't panic just yet," I told him. "Let's go down and check your room. Maybe she's in the shower or something."

Blaze nodded, then turned and rushed down the hall to his room. By the time we reached his door, I got an uneasy feeling when I saw there was no sign of Rip or Dane. We continued into Blaze's room, and again, there was no sign of anyone. "Damn. Where the hell could she be?"

"Maybe she got called into work," Gunner suggested.

"She would've messaged me."

Just when Blaze was about to lose it, Shadow and Riggs came walking up. "Everything okay?"

"No. Everything is *not okay*," Blaze barked. "I need to find Kenadee, and I need to find her right fucking now!"

Darcy

❦

As soon as Caleb left the room, I got up and took a shower. I'd just gotten dressed and was getting ready to leave when I got a text from a number I didn't recognize. I opened the message and was surprised to see that it was from Kenadee. She was letting me know that she and the other ol' ladies had decided not to postpone their monthly get-together after all. Instead, they were just meeting in the clubhouse kitchen, and she wanted me to join them. While I'd enjoyed hanging out with the girls the night before, I was feeling a little hesitant about meeting up with them again, especially after the way I'd overstepped with Gus. After mulling it over for a few minutes, I decided it would be best for me to just lay low for a little while, so I grabbed my stuff and headed towards the door. Just as I stepped into the hall, I heard someone call out my name. "Darcy!"

When I turned around, I found August walking in my direction. Unlike the night before, she was casually dressed in a pair of jeans and a t-shirt, and her hair was pulled back in a ponytail. "Hey, August. How's it going?"

"It's going good, I guess. I really need a cup of coffee."

I chuckled as I replied, "You and me both."

"Did you get Kenadee's message about breakfast?"

"I did, but I should probably pass."

"Oh, please don't. I'd really like you to come," she pleaded. "Besides, you said yourself you could use some coffee."

"I did, but—"

"It's just breakfast, Darcy," she interrupted. "It won't take long."

I let out a defeated sigh as I nodded. "Okay, I'll come, but let me throw this in my truck first."

"Great! I'll walk with you."

She followed me down the hall and out into the parking lot. When we got to my truck, I unlocked my door and tossed my bag into the passenger seat. As I closed the door, I noticed that August was standing several feet away, staring at my truck in complete awe. "I love your truck."

"Thanks." I locked the door and walked back towards her. "My grandfather gave it to me before he died, and I've been working on it ever since."

"Well, that does it. You're officially the coolest woman I've ever met."

"Oh, please. I'm far from cool," I argued.

"What? You're totally cool. Just look at you. Not only are you beautiful, but you're also extremely talented," she fussed. "I mean, seriously. From what I know, you're the only woman who's ever worked alongside the guys in the MC, and you're doing an incredible job. I'd say that makes you very cool."

Just as I was about to respond, Kenadee and Alex came barreling out of the back door of the clubhouse with

Gauge and Dane. Like August and me, both of the women were wearing their comfortable clothes—Kenadee had on a bright, hot pink t-shirt with loose-fit jeans, and Alex wore black leggings with an oversized rock band t-shirt. They were both talking a mile a minute, but stopped the minute she spotted August and me walking towards them. A bright smile crossed Kenadee's face. "Hey there, ladies. Are y'all coming to breakfast?"

"We're headed that way now."

"Great! We're going to make a quick run to get some more eggs and a gallon of milk. We'll be right back."

"Okay. We'll be waiting for ya."

They climbed into the SUV with Gauge, and seconds later they were pulling out of the parking lot. August and I were about to walk into the clubhouse when I happened to glance back to the road and noticed a familiar black Mercedes whipping out of the shadows. I stood there watching as it raced up behind Gauge's SUV and started following them. There was something about the whole scene that gave me an uneasy feeling. I was trying to figure out why it bothered me when August called, "Hey...you coming?"

"Yeah, I'm right behind ya."

I closed the door and followed her to the kitchen. I hadn't realized how hungry I was until I caught the scent of bacon and sausage on the stove. When we walked in, Reece and Riley were busy cooking while they talked to an older woman I'd never met before. It was clear from the sounds of their voices and the smiles on their faces that they were having a great time. The second Reece spotted us, she smiled and said, "Yay! You guys made it."

"Of course we did." August smiled. "We wouldn't miss it."

"Darcy, have you met August's mother, Samantha?"

"No, not yet." I walked over and shook her hand as I asked, "You and Gus are..."

"Yes." She smiled as she shook my hand. "It's nice to finally meet you. I've heard a lot of good things about you."

"Thanks, and I've heard a lot of great things about you too."

"Why don't you and August make yourselves some coffee? Kenadee and Alex went to get more eggs, but the pancakes should be ready in just a minute."

"Yeah, we just ran into them a couple of minutes ago." As I started towards the counter, I told her, "Coffee sounds great."

After August and I poured ourselves a cup, we checked to see if there was anything we could do to help, but from the looks of it, they had everything under control. As I looked down at all the food, I told them, "Wow, you guys have made quite a spread."

"We might've gotten a little carried away." Riley laughed as she pulled out a second tray of biscuits. "I figure the guys can eat the leftovers."

"Yeah, I'm sure they won't mind." Unable to resist, I grabbed a piece of bacon off the tray and took a bite. "It all looks so good."

"You want to help get all this to the table?"

"Sure."

I grabbed the platter of sausage and bacon, along with a tray of biscuits and carried them over to the table. August and Samantha brought over the pancakes and syrup while Reece and Riley grabbed the plates and silverware. When we had everything settled, we all sat down and just stared at the enormous amount of food. It wasn't long before Reece turned to Samantha and asked, "How much longer do you think Kenadee and Alex will be?"

"The store is just around the corner. I'd think they should be back any minute."

"Do you think they'd mind if we started without them?" Riley stared at the stack of pancakes as she continued, "I mean...it's hot, and it smells so good."

"I'm sure they wouldn't mind," Samantha replied. "I say we just go for it and beg for forgiveness later."

"Sounds good enough to me." Riley reached for a plate and added, "And if they get mad at us, we'll just blame Samantha."

"Hey, now!" Samantha fussed.

Riley put her arm around her as she smiled. "You know I'm just playing. We'd never throw you under the bus like that."

"Um-hmm," Samantha scoffed. "Sure, you wouldn't."

We all laughed as we each filled our plates. As we ate, the room was filled with the sounds of laughter and conversation, and I couldn't remember when I'd enjoyed myself more. These women were nothing like the girls I'd grown up with. They weren't judgmental or pretentious, and they treated one another with nothing but respect and kindness. Listening to them banter back and forth, I found myself wondering if I'd finally found a place where I wouldn't have to constantly keep my guard up while watching out for who might put the knife in my back. While I was skeptical, something told me I could be myself with these women, and it was a good feeling—a very good feeling. I was about to go for another pancake when Reece leaned over to me and asked, "So, what's the deal with you and Rider?"

"What do you mean?"

"I saw the way he was looking at you last night." She gave me a knowing look as she nudged me. "Pretty sure you were looking at him the same way."

"It's kind of complicated."

"It always is," she scoffed. "Rider is a good guy. The guys think a lot of him."

"Yeah, I think he's pretty great too. Always have."

"So, you two didn't just meet?"

"No. Actually, we kind of grew up together. We were pretty close when we were little, but we kind of drifted apart." I shrugged. "Like I said, it's complicated."

"Sometimes, it's us who make things complicated." She finished off her coffee then added, "But I'm sure you two will figure it out."

"Maybe. I guess we will see." I glanced over at the clock and was surprised that almost thirty minutes had passed since we'd started eating. Concerned, I looked over to Samantha and asked, "Shouldn't Kenadee and Alex be back by now?"

"You're right." Concerned, she reached into her pocket and took out her phone. "I better call and check on them."

We all watched in silence as she dialed the number and were startled when the sound of Kenadee's ringtone rang behind us. I'd heard it ring several times while we were eating, but didn't think much of it until now. There was no missing the concern in Riley's voice as she said, "I'll try to get Gauge."

All eyes were on Riley as she dialed his number and waited for him to answer. When he didn't, she shook her head and asked, "Do you think something's wrong?"

"I don't know," Reece answered as she stood up from the table. "Either way, I think it's time to let the guys know what's going on."

With all of us following close behind, she darted out of the kitchen and down the hall. We didn't get far before we ran into Blaze, Gunner, and Caleb. As soon as I saw their faces, I was hit with an uneasy feeling. I had no idea what was going on, but there was no doubt that it wasn't good. Blaze's tone was frantic as he asked, "Have you seen Kenadee?"

"We were just about to ask you the same," Riley answered. "She and Alex went with Gauge and Dane for a quick grocery run about thirty minutes ago. It shouldn't have taken them more than ten or fifteen minutes to get there and back, but there's been no sign of them. We tried calling them, but they didn't answer their phones. We were hoping—"

"Fuck," Blaze roared.

Caleb stepped forward and asked, "What about Alex? Have you tried reaching her?"

"No," Riley answered. "Let me try her now."

She dialed her number, and after several seconds, she said, "Alex...are you okay?" Only a few seconds passed before she started calling her name again, "Alex! Can you hear me? Are you okay?"

Her eyes widened as she looked over to Blaze and said, "The line went dead."

"Fuck."

"Do you have any idea which grocery store they were going to?" Caleb asked.

"We thought the one around the corner, but I don't know for sure," Reece answered.

Gunner turned to Blaze as he said, "We need to get Riggs. He can track their phones and figure out where the hell they are."

"I'll get him while you two go find Gus. Tell him what's

going on, and I'll let you know if Riggs is able to locate them."

"You got it."

When Blaze turned to leave, Caleb stepped over to me and said, "I'm sorry, but I need to—"

"Go," I interrupted. "Do what you gotta do."

"I'll come find you when we get this thing sorted."

"Actually, I...uh...I think I'm going to head on home. We can just catch up later."

"No." Worry crossed his eyes as he placed his hand on my arm. "You need to stay here until we know what the hell is going on."

"Why?"

"I don't have time to explain, Darcy." He let out a huff. "Hang out with the girls. Go back to my room. Whatever. Just stay put until I can get back to you."

I could tell from his expression there wasn't any point in arguing, so I nodded. "Okay. I'll stay."

He gave my arm a squeeze and seconds later, he was gone. I stood there for several moments with Reece and the others in a daze, then, without saying a word, we each made our way back to the kitchen. Everyone remained silent, each lost in her own world of thoughts while we started to clear the plates off the table and put them in the dishwasher. I had a million questions going through my head, but remembering what Caleb had told me about asking club-related questions, I decided to keep them to myself. It wasn't easy, especially when I overheard Riley and Reece talking to one another as they finished putting the leftovers in the fridge.

"Do you think this has anything to do with that guy who threatened Kenadee?" Riley asked with fear in her voice.

"I don't know, but from the way Blaze was freaking out, it makes me wonder." Reece inched closer to Riley as she continued, "I probably shouldn't say anything, but I overheard Riggs talking to Gunner the other day. I can't remember exactly what was said, but I think the guy they're worried about is the leader of some gang in town."

"Not that I'd know the difference, but do you have any idea which one?"

She shrugged. "It was something religious, like the Saints or the Disciples, but I can't say for sure."

As soon as she mentioned the Disciples, my mind drifted back to the day KeShawn Lewis had come to see Maybell. I could still remember the bitterness in his voice when he talked about avenging his son's murder. I had no doubt that he meant every word he'd said, and it chilled me right to the bone. I was going over our conversation in my head when I remembered he was driving a black Mercedes—just like the one I'd seen earlier in the morning when it appeared out of nowhere and started to follow Gauge's SUV. I couldn't imagine what Kenadee possibly had to do with his death, but there was no denying the fact that it was one hell of a coincidence. I wanted to ask them if I was right about my suspicions, but then I heard Riley say, "I know they're just trying to protect us, but I wish they'd just tell us something."

"Something tells me that isn't going to change any time soon."

When we finished cleaning up the last few dishes, Reece suggested that we all go down to the family room to wait on the guys. Everyone agreed, and it wasn't long before I found myself in a room filled with oversized sofas and chairs, a flat-screen TV over the fireplace, and several pool tables. As we all sat down and tried to get comfortable, I couldn't help but notice how much our little group's mood had changed. Less than an hour before, we were all talking and laughing, having ourselves a great time, but now everyone was completely silent. The longer I sat there, thinking about KeShawn and his promise of revenge, the more anxious I became. I couldn't shake the feeling that I needed to tell someone about the previous conversation we'd had and that I'd also seen his car following Gauge earlier, but I was so worried that I might be crossing some imaginary line set by the brothers that I just sat there and quietly waited with the others, praying it wouldn't be long before the guys returned with Kenadee and Alex.

Rider

Tensions were high and only growing as we waited for Riggs to pinpoint Kenadee and Alex's location. He was the club's hacker and we all knew that he had the skillset to find them, but with each second that passed, Shadow and Blaze were growing more and more impatient. The two were practically breathing down his neck as they watched him hammer away at his keyboard, the tension radiating off of them as they tried their damnedest to keep it together. Thankfully, it didn't take Riggs long to find their position. Once he confirmed that the cellphone was located at the nearby grocery store, we drove straight there in hopes of finding out what the fuck was going on.

The second we pulled up to the old, rundown store, there was no sign of Gauge's SUV, but that didn't stop Blaze and Shadow from jumping out and rushing inside to see if they could locate Kenadee and Alex. When we raced in after them, Glen, the old man who ran the store, came to the door. His face was pale and sweat was trickling down his forehead as he pointed and said, "You need to get around back. Hurry."

I nodded, then turned to Riggs. "Get in your truck and drive around back."

As soon as he headed towards the SUV, Gunner and I took off towards the back of the grocery store, and I was totally unprepared for what I found. Gauge's SUV was parked next to the back door, and as I got closer, I could hear someone huffing and puffing as they dragged something across the ground. I continued towards the sound, but stopped when Alex came rushing out of the back door covered in blood with an armful of towels. Her face was riddled with panic as she hurried to the back of the truck and said, "Here are some more towels."

Gunner and I raced over to see what was going on and froze as we looked down and saw Gauge and Alex hovering over Dane, pressing towels against his chest. Neither one was aware that we were standing behind them as Gauge shouted, "Fuck, you're gonna have to get a hold of the brothers."

I knelt down and pressed a towel against one of Dane's wounds. "We're here, brother. It's going to be okay."

When Blaze and Shadow came barreling out of the back door, Alex stood and rushed over to Shadow, wrapping her arms tightly around his neck. "Thank God, you're finally here."

"Are you okay?" Shadow asked as he pulled her close.

"I am now," she cried. "I've been trying to call you, but I couldn't get through. Kenadee—"

"What about Kenadee?" Blaze roared. "Where the fuck is she?"

"I don't know." Alex's voice trembled as she looked over to Blaze and said, "It all happened so fast. They took her."

"Who took her?"

"*The Disciples*," Glen answered for her.

"Are you sure?" Blaze pushed.

"Yes, son. I'm sure." Since his store was so close to the clubhouse, we'd stopped by many times. Over the years, we'd gotten to know Glen as a man we could trust. "I saw the gang stamp on one of their necks."

"Dammit!" Gauge was doing what he could to help Dane, but it wasn't enough. Panicked, he looked up at Shadow and said, "We need to get him to Mack before he loses any more blood."

Mack was the club's doctor, in charge of tending to all the brothers' medical needs—from simple coughs to gunshot wounds. After serving as a medic in the Marines, there wasn't much he hadn't dealt with. As Shadow started towards them, he ordered, "Let's move."

It wasn't until we started to lift him off the ground when I noticed that Dane wasn't the only one who was wounded. "Damn, brother. You've been hit."

"I'm fine."

After I saw the amount of blood Gauge was losing from bullet wounds in his shoulder and thigh, I argued, "No, you're not."

Showing that he wasn't the least bit concerned about himself, he shook his head and said, "Told ya. I'm fine."

I didn't argue. Instead, I helped the others get Dane into the back of Gunner's SUV. There was no missing the concern in Gauge's voice as he urged, "We need to hurry. He's running out of time."

With that, we all piled in the SUV and rushed Dane to the clubhouse. As soon as we were parked, Shadow took Alex to his room to get cleaned up, while we got Dane and Gauge down to the infirmary. When we walked in, Gus and Moose, along with several of the other brothers, were already there waiting for us. They could all see that Dane was hanging by a thread as we carried him into one of the med rooms and lay him down on the gurney. Mack rushed over, and a look of concern crossed his face as he started to assess his wounds. We all knew it was bad. We'd all seen that Dane's clothes were completely soaked in blood and how he'd been barely able to keep his eyes open, but it wasn't too long ago that Mack had brought Gunner back from death's door. I just hoped that he'd be able to do the same for Dane.

Wasting no time, Gus went over to Gauge and asked, "What the hell happened?"

"I fucked up, Prez. I don't know what I was thinking." Anguish crossed his face as he continued, "I told both Kenadee and Alex that they didn't need more eggs, but Kenadee wouldn't let it go. She kept saying that it would only take a few minutes...that they'd run in and run out. No big deal. I finally gave in, and Dane and I took them over to Glen's place."

"So, you got there. What happened after that?" Gus pushed.

"Since they were just going for some eggs and milk, I figured it would only take a minute, so I just pulled up to the door." Gauge shook his head and continued, "Sent Dane inside with them and waited on them to come back. Such a stupid fucking move. I should've gone in too. If I had, none of this shit would've happened."

"Gauge." Gus's tone was firm, but compassionate. "I'm gonna need you to pull it together, brother. We gotta know what happened after the girls went inside the store."

Gauge nodded. "Those assholes must've been watching...followed us there or something, 'cause I'd only been waiting there but a couple of minutes when I heard gunshots. I went straight inside, and Glen motioned me to the back of the store. That's where I found Dane and Alex laid out on the ground. Dane was still conscious and told me how the two guys came up behind them, knocking Alex out and shooting him before going after Kenadee. She tried to get away, but she just wasn't fast enough. They carried her out the back, and I never saw a goddamn thing."

I looked over to Gus and said, "Glen saw them. Confirmed it was the Disciples."

"Damn."

"As soon as he saw what was going down, Glen closed the store. Tried to give us time to get cleared out before anyone knew what was happening."

"We owe him for that," Gus replied. "We've got to see if we can figure out where they took Kenadee. You stay put and let Mack fix you up."

"I'm sorry, Prez. This is all on me. I should've—"

"Can't dwell on that right now, brother. What's done is done. Right now, you focus on getting these wounds tended to."

"Yes, sir."

While we all wanted to stay there and make sure both of our brothers were going to be okay, we didn't have that option. We not only had to find Kenadee, but also figure out a way to get her back before Lewis did something stupid. After Gus whispered something to Mack, he turned and motioned for us to follow as he headed out the door. We all gathered in the conference room and set to work on finding Kenadee. Without her phone to trace, we were limited to the security cameras that Riggs had installed over near Lewis's place a few days earlier. Unfortunately, they weren't much help.

"I just don't know," Riggs huffed with frustration. "His car is there, but the place looks pretty quiet. Doesn't look like anyone is coming or going."

"Can you back the feed up...see what was going on half an hour ago?" Moose asked.

"Yeah. Give me a minute." After a few keystrokes on his laptop, he was able to rewind the feed, and as soon as he noticed that the car hadn't been in the driveway a few minutes earlier, he stopped the feed, slowly moving it frame by frame until he spotted his car. "You guys seeing this?"

We all looked up at the monitor on the wall and watched as Lewis' black Mercedes crept up to the back of the house. Because of the distance from the cameras and the fenced-in backyard, we didn't have a clear view of what was going on. We could see a good deal of movement, several people came in and out of the house, but that was it. Just as Riggs started to zoom in, Blaze shouted, "Hold up!"

"You see something?"

"Yeah. Go back a couple of frames." Riggs started to reverse the feed, and after several seconds, he slammed his hand down on the table. "Damn. It was nothing."

"Yeah, that fucking fence is making it pretty hard to tell what the hell is going on over there," Riggs added as he tried to zoom in closer.

"You know, we're gonna have to change the plan." Gus ran his hand over his beard as he said, "There's no way we can go in there tonight...not like this. Lewis has at least ten guys holed up in that house. We're gonna need a good deal of gun power to take them out. Right now, we have no idea where he's keeping Kenadee, and if we aren't careful, we'll be putting her in harm's way. We can't take the chance."

"But we gotta do something, Prez," Blaze urged. "If she's there with him, there's no telling what he'll do."

"We'll figure it out, brother. One way or another, we'll get her out of there," he assured him. "Riggs, we gotta get eyes inside that house. We've got to know where he's holding her."

"I've been trying, but there's always somebody at his place." He shook his head with frustration. "Haven't been able to get inside without being seen, and now that they have Kenadee, I don't see that changing any time soon."

Frustrations were building by the second. Hell, I could feel the tension radiating off my brothers and me, crackling around the room like a fucking electrical storm. We needed a break, and we needed it bad. The only bit of good news we'd had during the hours we'd been meeting was the fact that Mack had been able to stabilize Dane, and he'd patched up Gauge. While they were both going to pull through, the fact that our brothers had been wounded by the Disciples made us even more determined to take them down. We were all were trying to come up with some kind of plan when there was a knock on the conference room door. No one ever disturbed us when we were in a meeting, so at first it was completely ignored. But then, there was a second knock—much louder than the first. All eyes turned to the door as Gus got up and opened it, slowly revealing Darcy standing on the other side. I knew the second I saw that look of apprehension on her face that things were about to go from bad to worse. Fuck.

Darcy

I'd been sitting in that family room with the others for what seemed like hours when Gunner messaged August and told her that they'd found Alex. He said she was safe and sound but didn't mention much else. We were all left wondering about Kenadee and whether or not she was okay. The *not knowing* was eating at all of us. Unfortunately, there was nothing we could do but sit there and wait which wasn't one of my strong suits. I was beyond impatient, and with my overactive imagination, I was becoming more anxious by the minute. I couldn't stop thinking about the conversation I'd overheard between Reece and Riley. There was no way I could be sure, but I couldn't shake the feeling that KeShawn Lewis was behind Kenadee's disappearance, and it terrified me. From the first time I'd met the guy, I knew that he was bad news, and when I learned that he was the leader of the Disciples, I quickly realized that I was right to be leery of him. They were always on the news for causing some kind of trouble, from shootouts to robberies, and that was just the start. If I was right, and he really was involved in all this, then I feared the MC was gonna have to pull out all the stops to get Kenadee back.

I wanted to do something, *anything* to help them get her back, but I didn't have a clue as to what that could be. I thought about it and thought about, then, out of the blue, it hit me. Without thinking it all through, I got up from the sofa and asked the girls, "Where would the guys be right now?"

"The conference room, I guess." Reece shrugged as she continued, "At least, that's where they usually meet when something's going on."

"Okay. Where's the conference room?"

"It's just down the hall on the right. Why?"

As I started towards the door, I told her, "I'll explain later."

"Darcy, wait!" Reece shouted. "You can't go in there while they're meeting."

Ignoring her warning, I continued down the hall and stopped when I got to the large wooden double doors on the right. I paused for a moment, taking a deep breath as I considered what I was about to do. After I mustered up the courage, I knocked on the door and waited several seconds, but no one answered. I knocked a second time, harder than before, and when I heard footsteps coming in my direction, a wave of apprehension washed over me as the door opened. As soon as I saw the look on Gus's face, my mind went blank, and I was suddenly at loss for words. "Darcy? You need something?"

I nodded. "I know I'm not supposed to ask questions, and I won't, but...umm...I think I might be able to help with finding Kenadee."

"Oh, really? How's that?"

Before I could answer, Caleb came over to the door,

and with a harsh tone, he growled, "You can't be here, Darcy!"

"I knew you were going to say that." I sighed. "But—"

"But nothing. What the hell are you doing here?"

"I came to talk to you about Kenadee."

Clearly furious that I was there and had interrupted his meeting with his brothers, he leaned towards me with a scowl. "We've got it covered, Darcy. You need to go."

"But I think I might be able to help."

"I just told you. We've got it covered."

"Fine, I just thought you might want some help getting close to KeShawn Lewis." I looked at both of them, studying their facial expressions for some sign that I was wrong about my suspicions, but neither of them so much as flinched. I knew then that I was right. "But if you've got it covered, I'll be on my way."

When I turned and started back down the hall, I heard Blaze shout, "Hold up! Let's hear her out."

"Darcy, wait." When I turned back around, Blaze had come up next to Caleb and Gus, eagerly waiting as Caleb said, "Say what you came here to say."

"Okay." I stepped back over to them and tried to keep myself calm. "If I'm right about KeShawn Lewis and his Disciples having something to do with whatever happened to Kenadee, I might be able to help."

"First...what makes you think that Lewis has anything to do with this?" Gus asked.

"I overheard something one of the ol' ladies said." I shrugged. "That, and I saw his car this morning."

"When did you see his car?" Blaze asked.

"When I went out with August to put my bag in my truck. We were on our way back inside when I spotted his black Mercedes following Gauge's SUV."

Blaze snarled, "And you didn't say anything."

"Why would I? I had no idea that he was causing problems for y'all!"

Gus's eyes narrowed as he asked, "How do you know he drives a black Mercedes?"

"His grandmother and I live in the same trailer park, and he comes by from time to time to check on her." Making sure he didn't think I was trying to hide something, I looked him right in the eye as I continued, "The last time he was there, I noticed he was driving a black Mercedes with both a rear and roof spoiler and aftermarket rims."

"And you saw the same vehicle this morning?"

"Yes, sir. I did."

There was no missing the look of concern on Gus's face as stood there going over what I'd just said. After several moments passed, he finally looked back to me and said, "So, how exactly is it that you think you can help us, Darcy?"

"The last time KeShawn came to see his grandmother, he mentioned that he had a Suzuki GSX-R he wanted to have painted and asked if I would check it out." I glanced over at Caleb. "I told him I'd need to see it first, so he gave me his number and address. He wanted me to come by his house to see what I thought."

"And how exactly does this help us with our situation?"

"I could go over there and tell him that I've come to see about painting his bike," I explained. "While I'm there, I can take a look around for any sign of Kenadee."

"No fucking way you're going over to that house." Caleb's eyes lit up with rage as he stared down at me. "Not now. Not ever."

"So, you have a better idea in mind?" I asked sarcastically.

"Doesn't matter. It's too fucking dangerous!"

I placed my hands on my hips as I argued, "You aren't even going to consider it as an option?"

"Not a time for your stubborn bullshit, Darcy!"

"We need to at least consider this," Blaze told him.

"I said no." His tone changed when he turned to Gus. "We can't send her over there, Prez. You said it yourself, this guy was a loose cannon, and we don't know for certain that Kenadee is even there."

As soon as the words left his mouth, I pushed, "You would know if you just let me go check it out."

Caleb stared back at me with one of his warning looks, and I knew right then that my stubborn, snarky side was about to get me in trouble. I needed to rein it in before I said something I would regret, so I inhaled a deep breath and tried to collect myself as I waited for Gus's response. I could see the wheels spinning in his head as he turned and looked at Riggs. He pondered a moment more, then brought his attention back to me. "Gonna need you to give us some time to talk this over."

Realizing that he was trying to get rid of me, I nodded. "Okay, I'll be in Caleb's room if you need me."

As I started down the hall, I thought Caleb might come after me; instead, I heard the large doors of the conference room close behind me. I was more than a little curious about what they might be saying, and I had to fight the urge to rush back over to the doors and eavesdrop. I knew it was a bad idea, so I decided against it and continued on to Caleb's room. As soon as I walked in, I crawled into his bed and pulled the covers over me. I was immediately enveloped in his scent, and it wasn't long before my mind drifted to the night before. With everything that had been going on, I hadn't had a chance to really stop and think about it, much less make sense of it. I knew I was attracted to him. Hell, with his good looks, there wasn't a woman in a fifty-mile radius who wouldn't find him desirable, but there was so much more to my attraction towards him than just his looks. The way he spoke, the way he smelled, and the way he looked at me like I was the only woman in the world set off a spark inside of me, burning through me from the inside out. I didn't know it was possible to feel the kind of passion I felt when I was in his arms, which only made me want him even more.

I shouldn't have been surprised that our night together was so amazing. When we were kids, things always came so easy with Caleb and me. We could just be ourselves, never thinking about what we should or shouldn't say or how we should act with one another. Back then, it seemed so simple. I'd even fantasized about Caleb and me falling in love. In some random moment, we'd suddenly realize that there was something more between us than just a friendship, and we'd become high school sweethearts. We'd go on dates, hold hands and make out, and even go to prom together. All those little fantasies died the day I decided to protect my heart and walk away from our friendship. I thought I'd lost my chance forever, but I was wrong. I felt that same connection I'd always felt for Caleb the moment I saw him standing in that garage, but I'd been too blind to see that he was feeling it too. There was no denying it now—not after the night we'd shared and his reaction to me going to KeShawn's place. It was clear that he felt just as strongly about me as I did him.

I was still going over it all in my head when my cellphone rang. It was rare for me to get calls, especially since I'd moved away from home, so I thought it might be Caleb trying to reach me. I quickly pulled it from my pocket, and dread washed over me when I saw it was my brother, Eddie. I never heard from my brothers unless they needed something, and I had a feeling that this time was no different. "Hey, Eddie."

"Hey, sis! How's it going?" he asked in a chipper voice.

"It's going." I tried to brace myself as I asked, "What do you need?"

"Can't I just call to check on my little sister?"

"You could, but you never do." Even though neither of them had ever given me any reason to, I loved both of my brothers. After my mother ran out on us, they were the only real family I had, so I always tried to do what I could to help them out when I could—even if it meant forking over all of my rent money to bail them out of jail or to square them up with their drug dealers. "So, what is it that you need, Eddie?"

"Well, I ran into a little trouble last night and got myself locked up. I'm gonna need you to come down to the police station on Main and bail me out."

"Sorry, but I can't today." There was no way I could tell him the truth—not that he'd believe me if I did. "I'm kind of tied up right now."

"Get untied up, Darcy!" he fussed. "I ain't got nobody else I can call to come get me out of this joint."

"You should've thought about that before you got yourself locked up." I knew spouting off was only going to cause him to do the same, so I quickly rebounded by saying, "I'd help out if I could, but I just can't do it today. Do you want me to try to get in touch with Danny and see if he can head over there?"

"No point in that."

"Why not?"

"He's in the fucking cell next to me, so he won't be much help," he scoffed.

"Damn."

I let out a deep breath as I tried to think of some other option. Before I could come up with something, Eddie said, "Look. Don't worry about it. We'll figure something out."

"You sure?"

"Yeah. Danny's still got a call. Maybe he can find someone who owes him a favor."

"Okay. I'm sorry I couldn't help."

"Don't sweat it. We'll be fine," he assured me.

I couldn't help but feel a little guilty after the call ended. It was the first time I hadn't been there for them when they needed me, but there wasn't anything I could do. There was no way I was going to walk away from Caleb and the rest of his brothers when there was a chance I could help them get Kenadee back. Besides, there was always the possibility that a couple of nights in jail might make them think before they did something stupid again. I tried to hold on to that hope as I put my phone back in my pocket and lay back down on the bed.

Rider

✿

"Are we sure that we can even trust this girl?" Gus asked with concern. "Seems odd that she has this kind of connection to Lewis."

"When I did her background check, I found no ties to him or anyone else that seemed suspicious. Her brothers are both trouble, but with dumb shit like dope and fighting in bars. No gang association whatsoever." Riggs turned to me as he said, "And Rider can vouch for her...They have history. Grew up in Oakland together."

"We can trust her," I replied with confidence. "You have my word on that."

"Good." Gus thought for a moment, then said, "Now, the only question is when we send her in."

"I don't know, brother. I think we've gotta wait...at least for a little while," Moose told Gus. "Darcy waltzes in there right now, not but a few hours after he's taken Kenadee, and he's gonna smell a rat."

"He's right," Riggs agreed. "He's never gonna believe it's a coincidence if she shows up there about that fucking bike."

"So, what do you suggest?"

"We send her first thing in the morning," Moose answered. "Give things a minute to settle down."

"And what about Kenadee?" Blaze barked. "We're just supposed to sit back and wait on this motherfucker to kill her?"

"If he was going to kill her, he would've already done it." Shadow looked him directly in the eye, trying his best to assure his brother and best friend that his ol' lady would be okay. "He could've killed her at the store, but he didn't. There's a reason for that."

"And what reason would that be?"

"If he's smart, he'll plan on using her as bait to get to us. Plain and simple." Shadow leaned forward as he continued, "There's just one problem. He's going to be dead long before that can ever happen."

"We've just got to be smart, brother," Riggs added. "We need to get his numbers down. If the Red Knights have tied up with him, then I say we go after them first. Take them out before Lewis has any clue that we know they're in cahoots."

"We just going to show up at their hangout and wipe them out?" T-Bone asked.

"No. That would draw too much attention. We don't want to tip Lewis off. I think going after them individually is our safest bet." Riggs never ceased to amaze me. Not only was the guy brilliant when it came to computers, but he was also a master at thinking outside of the box. "We hit them at home, the streets, or at their fucking hangouts, and one by one we end these motherfuckers before they have a chance to team up with the Disciples."

"How are we going to find all these assholes?"

"Shadow will take care of that," Gus assured him. "He

still has Bonds in one of his holding rooms, and with a little pressing, he'll give us the names we need."

"And after we've dealt with the Red Knights, then we hit Lewis's place?" Blaze pushed.

"You got it." Gus nodded. "We'll take care of him and whatever crew he's got holed up there as soon as Darcy gets those cameras planted and we can see what the hell is going on in there."

"So, Darcy goes to Lewis's place first thing in the morning," Blaze started. "She'll use painting his bike or whatever as a way of getting her foot in the door. Then, when he isn't looking, she'll plant the cameras and mics throughout the house."

"That's it."

It sounded like a solid plan, but none of them had mentioned the fact that we were putting Darcy's life in danger. One wrong move, and I'd lose her. I couldn't stand the thought, so after keeping my mouth shut as long as I could, I finally said, "So, we're going to send Darcy into the lion's den...*alone*—with no gun or way of protecting herself, and just keep our fingers crossed that she doesn't end up with a fucking bullet in her head?"

"Darcy's a smart girl, Rider. She knows how to handle herself."

"And we'll be using a radio transmitter so we can talk her through it," Riggs explained. "From the minute she walks through that door, I'll be right there with her, and if something goes wrong, we'll be there waiting."

"What aren't you getting? She'll still be in that house alone with Lewis!"

"Lewis has done his homework, and he knows who is and isn't a brother of Satan's Fury." Riggs shook his head.

"No way any of us can go in there with her without him knowing."

"What about Clay?" Moose suggested. "Why couldn't he go with her? Pretend to be her boyfriend or something."

"Hadn't considered that." Gus thought for a moment. "Might be a chance for him to prove whether or not he's got what it takes to prospect."

I knew better than to question Gus, but sending Clay in with Darcy didn't make me feel any better about things. He was good guy, tried hard, but the kid was green. Since I'd never seen him in a situation like this, I was concern that he wouldn't know how to handle himself with men like Lewis. Hell, if he hadn't been around gangs before, they'd scare the shit out of him, but then again, that might play out to be an advantage. If he looked freaked out, then maybe, just maybe, Lewis would actually believe that he was simply Darcy's boyfriend and nothing more. We talked a few more minutes, then Gus sent Shadow to start working on Bonds while Riggs went to his office to see what he could find out. While they were both busy working to find all the members of the Disciples, he and I went to talk to Darcy. When we walked into my room, she was curled up in the covers on my bed like a cocoon, and for a moment, I thought she might be asleep. "Darcy?"

She pulled the covers down to look at me, and her eyes widened with surprise when she saw that Gus was standing there next to me. "Oh, hey!"

As she unwound the covers and sat up in the bed, I told her, "We need to talk."

"Okay." She quickly stood as she asked, "What about?"

Gus stepped forward as he looked down at her and

said, "About going over to KeShawn Lewis's place. We think you might be able to help us after all."

"Okay, great. What do you need me to do?"

Her eyes narrowed as Gus told her, "First, I want to make sure you know that you don't have to do this. It'll be dangerous going over there. On a good day, Lewis isn't a man I'd ever trust. He's short fused and acts before he thinks, so there's no way for any of us to know how he'll react to you showing up over there."

"I know, but I think I'll be okay," she assured him. "Just let me know what you need me to do."

Gus took a few minutes to explain everything to her. She seemed fine with Riggs fitting her with a radio trans-mitter and that Clay would be tagging along, but I didn't miss the flash of unease that crossed her face when he brought up the cameras and microphones. Darcy was a smart woman. She knew it wouldn't be easy to get into Lewis's house, much less planting the cameras without being caught by one of his crew. It was a big risk, one that I didn't want her to take, but it was the only way. Once he was done going through everything, Gus asked, "Do you think you can handle all that?"

"Yes, sir." She hesitated for just a half-second, then continued, "I can do it. No problem."

"Good. I'll let the others know." As Gus started for the door, he glanced back and said, "Be ready to head out first thing in the morning."

"I'll be ready."

As soon as he walked out of the room, I stepped over to her and asked, "Are you sure you want to go through with this?"

"I'll admit I have my concerns, but they aren't enough to stop me from doing it." Her eyes met mine. "Besides, if the roles were reversed, Kenadee would do the same for me."

Before I even realized what I was doing, I'd reached for her, pulling her towards me as I wrapped my arms around her. As I stood there holding her, I couldn't stop thinking about her being in harm's way. I wanted to protect her, keep her safe, yet I was allowing her to be put in danger. The thought ate at me, making me wonder if I was making a huge mistake by letting her go through with this thing. "I'm going to need you to be careful, *very careful*."

"I will be." She nestled her head against my shoulder as she hugged me back. "You don't have to worry. I'll be fine."

"I'm going to hold you to that, 'cause I don't know what I'd do if something happened to you."

Darcy looked at me for a brief moment, studying me with a soul-searching stare, then lifted up on her tiptoes and pressed her mouth to mine. Damn. She felt so fucking good in my arms, better than I could've ever imagined. Needing more, my hand slipped to the nape of her neck and tugged at her hair, guiding her mouth towards mine. A light moan escaped from her throat as I delved deeper, my tongue tangling with hers. It wasn't long before we were both lost in the kiss. Without thinking, my hands dropped to the hem of her t-shirt, and I'd just pulled it over her head when there was a knock at my door. There was no missing the frustration in my voice as I called, "Yeah!"

"Need you back in the conference room."

"I'm on my way." I lowered my mouth to Darcy's ear, softly trailing kisses below her ear before I whispered, "We'll have to finish this later."

"Okay." When I released her and started for the door, she asked, "How long do you think you'll be?"

"Can't say for sure. Just make yourself comfortable, and I'll be back as soon as I can."

"Okay. Just be careful."

I nodded. "Always."

I walked out of the room, closed the door, and started back to the conference room. When I walked in, I was surprised to see that Shadow and Riggs had both returned and were standing up front with Gus. As soon as I found my seat, Shadow started passing out folders with names and photographs of each of the Disciple's members. "Turns out the Red Knights have twenty-one members. We managed to get all their photo IDs and possible locations of where they can be found. If we can cover our tracks and remain off radar, we shouldn't have a problem wiping out these fuckers by the end of the night."

"Are we waiting until nightfall, or are we doing this thing now?" T-Bone asked.

"The sooner the better," Riggs answered. "I know it would be easier to lay low at night, but time isn't on our side. We need to move while we know where we can find these guys."

"Understood."

Gus looked out at us as he said, "Shadow and Riggs will break you into groups and give you all the information on your targets. We need to move fast on this. Get the job done and get the hell out of there."

We all nodded.

"We're keeping this whole thing low profile," Shadow announced. "No cuts or bikes today, fellas. Take the SUVs and don't leave any evidence behind. I want each of you in direct contact with me at all times. Nobody makes a move without checking in first. Understood?"

All the guys responded in unison. "Understood."

"Once you have your assignments from Shadow, get geared up and let us know when you head out," Gus ordered.

Shadow and Riggs started passing out information to each of the different groups. As soon as Gunner, T-Bone, and I had our list of names and addresses, we went to the garage to gather a couple of extra weapons and ammo. We were all silent, each preparing for what was to come on our own, as we each grabbed a couple of our old .22 revolvers. They didn't leave an exit wound, so there would be less mess, especially if we were able to get close—really close. Once we'd loaded up with extra ammunition and a few thick plastic bags, we radioed in to Gus to let him know we were on our way out. With T-Bone behind the wheel, we set off for downtown, and fifteen minutes later, we were pulling across the street to the backside of our first address. The worn-down house was on a main street right in the middle of the hood, making it difficult to advance without being seen. As he killed the engine, T-Bone turned around and offered me a baseball cap. "You got your silencer on?"

"Yeah." I threw the hat on my head. "I'm set."

"I'll go first. We'll go in through the back," T-Bone explained. "Keep your head down and let's get this thing done."

As soon as he got out of the truck, my pulse started racing as Gunner and I followed him up to the back door. The two of us watched in silence as T-Bone took a quick look through the window, then glanced back to make sure that we were ready. We gave him the nod, and seconds later, he was reaching for the doorknob. Thankfully, it was unlocked, and we were able to enter without breaking down the door. While we'd been in situations like this before, it was impossible not to feel anxious as we stepped inside. T-Bone held up his hand, and we all immediately froze when we heard voices coming from the next room. Our target was just a few feet away, but he wasn't alone. We could only hope that the others were also members, and we could take out more than one while we were there.

As I waited for T-Bone to give the okay to advance, I took a quick look around the kitchen, and my stomach turned at the filth: dirty dishes piled up in the sink, the garbage can overflowed, and roaches covered the walls. After several moments, T-Bone eased up to the doorway for a better look, then turned back to us with a nod. With my gun drawn, I followed as he started into the next room. When we walked in, three men were sitting on the sofa smoking pot. The big guy on the end caught my eye first. He had a dragon tattoo that started at his back and made its way up to his neck, stopping just as it reached his cheek. I had no doubt that he was one of the guys in the photographs Riggs and Shadow had shown us, and the guy next to him looked familiar as well. The third guy I wasn't so sure about. He was thin with no ink that I could see, but it was hard to tell with all the smoke billowing around him.

They continued to banter back and forth, completely oblivious to the fact that we were we standing right behind them. T-Bone took another step forward and placed the barrel of his gun against the big guy's head. His voice was low and full of warning as he said, "I'm gonna need you assholes to shut the fuck up before I blow your brains all over the fucking ceiling."

Silence filled the room as each of them slowly turned their heads to look at us. It wasn't until then that I could see just how blitzed they really were. The one in the middle finally mumbled, "What da fuck, man. What you doing in my crib?"

"Word on the street is you and your boys planning something with the Disciples."

He shrugged. "What's it to you?"

"We want to know what Lewis did with the girl?"

His brows furrowed as he asked, "Who the fuck is Lewis?"

"Slayer," T-Bone growled. "Now, what the fuck did he do with the girl?"

"I don't know nothing about no girl," he lied.

T-Bone ground his gun into the back of the guy's head. "You sure about that?"

"I done told you. I don't know shit about no fucking girl!" he shouted as he pointed his finger across the room. "There's the fucking door. Now, get the fuck outta here before you end up dead!"

Knowing T-Bone like I did, I wasn't surprised when he decided against pushing the guy any further and simply grabbed a plastic bag from his back pocket and quickly slipped it over the guy's head. The asshole didn't have a chance to react before T-bone had pulled the trigger, killing him instantly. The other two freaked out and started shouting incoherently as they tried for their own weapons. Gunner and I quickly stepped into action, placing the barrel of our guns at their temples, and they both froze. After several deep breaths, the guy with the tattoo started, "We don't know where he put the girl, man. I swear it. We just got word that he got her. That's it."

"What else do you know?"

"What do you want to know?" he gasped.

"Everything you know about Slayer's plan to take down

Satan's Fury, and it better be fucking good or you're fucking done," I growled.

"Just know he got that girl he's been after, and she's tied to their club." He glanced back at me with a grimace. "Tied to *your club*."

"And?"

"He offered us a shit-ton of guns and dope to help him hit you where it hurts."

I nudged him with my gun. "What the fuck is that supposed to mean?"

"He wants us to help him hit your garage and some diner too." Unlike Anthony, this guy wasn't worried about running his mouth, but that changed the minute his buddy gave him a warning look. Realizing that he was snitching, my guy's back stiffened, and he instantly stopped talking. Knowing he had more to tell, I looked over to Gunner, and reading my mind, he took a bag from his pocket and thrust it over the friend's head. Once he had it secured, I aimed my barrel at his head and pulled the trigger of my .22, killing him instantly. My guy panicked as he screamed, "What the fuck, man!"

"You're next unless you tell us everything you fucking know."

"Slayer knows where your president lives." His eyes dropped to the floor as he continued, "He's planning on taking him and his family out before coming after the rest of you."

It took all the restraint I could muster not to pull the trigger after I heard him say what Lewis was gonna try to do to Gus. I was too angry to even speak, so Gunner stepped forward. "When?"

"Hell, you never know with fucking Slayer. We could get the call tonight, or it can be next fucking week," he complained. "Besides, he's got the girl now. That's going to keep him entertained for a while."

"What the fuck is that supposed to mean?" Gunner barked.

"From what I've heard, he's been trying to get his hands on her for weeks. Now that he has her"—he shook his head with a smirk—"I figure he's going to have himself *a real good* time."

"I've heard enough," T-bone snarled. "End the motherfucker."

"Wait!" The guy raised his hands and started, "You said—"

Before he could finish his sentence, Gunner had put a bag over his head and stepped back as I squeezed the trigger. The job was done. As I looked down at the lifeless bodies in front of me, I quickly realized that killing them was the easy part. Now we had to figure out how to deal with the aftermath, which wouldn't be easy in the light of day. T-Bone pulled out his burner and called Gus to catch him up to speed. Once he got off the phone with him, he turned his attention to us. "We gotta get this mess cleaned up."

"You got any thoughts on how we're gonna do that in broad fucking daylight?" Gunner asked.

"I'd say we'd burn the place to the ground, but that will bring too much attention. We're gonna have to clean this shit up the best we can and find a place to dump the bodies."

"And how are we supposed to get them out of here without being seen?"

"I've got some bleach, gloves, and plastic tarps in the back of the truck. I'll go grab them," T-Bone answered as he headed towards the door. "We're gonna need to make sure we don't leave any trace of blood anywhere."

"You got it."

Once T-Bone returned with the plastic, we got busy wrapping each of the bodies. By the time we were done, T-bone had already backed the truck up to the rear-entry door and was ready to help us start loading them into the SUV. We were just about to carry the first body out when the sound of police sirens stopped me dead in my tracks. "What the fuck?"

"Don't sweat it. We're good," T-Bone assured me. "After I checked in with Gus, he had Riggs call in a false report of rape around the corner. That will keep our local nosey-bodies busy for a while."

"Good thinking."

In a matter of minutes, we had all the bodies loaded in the truck. Before we rolled, I went through the house once more, making sure we'd left nothing behind. After I was certain that all was clear, I went back out to the truck, and we started towards our next hit. Thankfully, he wasn't only easy to find, he was an easy kill. We were able to catch him stumbling out of a local bar. He was totally wasted and never saw us coming. Gunner and I had just loaded him in the back with the others when we got the call from Gus. It turned out that Riggs's plan worked. We'd wiped out the Red Knights, leaving nothing but the easily forgotten memory of their name behind, and it wouldn't be long before we'd do the same to the Disciples. KeShawn Lewis was about to learn the hard way why you don't go up against Satan's Fury, and you sure as hell don't fuck with their ol' ladies.

Darcy

❧

I was half asleep when I felt Caleb slip into bed next to me and wrap his arm around my waist. His body was still warm from a hot shower, and I could smell the fresh scent of soap when he nestled in behind me. I kept waiting for him to say something, but all I got was silence and the subtle heat of his breath at the back of my neck. He was so still and quiet, I might've thought he was sleeping, but I knew he wasn't. I could feel the tension radiating off of him as he lay there next to me, staring at the back of my head. I knew he was concerned about me going over to KeShawn's place, and I was too. I wasn't naïve enough to think he would just let me walk into his place without question, especially when he had Kenadee locked away in there, but I owed it to her and Blaze to at least try.

Since neither of us was getting any sleep, I decided to try and take his mind off of things for a little while and asked, "Do you remember that night you helped me fix that battery in my truck?"

"Yeah, I do."

"You remember how I asked you out?"

"Yeah, only after I asked you out and you turned me down," he teased.

"Asking if I wanted to go to some party wasn't asking me out," I argued. "But *anyway*. Did you know that I had this big night planned for us? I'd been working on my cousin's '72 GT, and I thought we could take it out on the track for a test run."

"That would've been incredible." The sadness in his voice tugged at my heart when he said, "I hope you know I would've been there if it hadn't been for the accident."

"I know." I rolled over to face him and placed the palm of my hand on his chest. "I really hate what happened to you. I can't imagine how hard it must've been for you to go through that."

"I was pretty bad, but I'm the one who made it harder than it needed to be."

"How so?"

"I let my bitterness get the best of me." He let out a deep breath. "Like I told you before, I did things I wasn't proud of. Got hooked on my pain meds, destroyed my family, and got myself kicked out. Hell, I almost died before I pulled my head out of my ass."

"We all make mistakes, Caleb."

"I didn't just make one mistake. I made a fucking truck load of them."

"Maybe so, but things seemed to have turned out okay for you now." I paused for a moment before asking, "What about your family? Have you worked things out?"

"I haven't spoken to them since the day they kicked me out."

"Oh." His answer surprised me. Caleb's folks were good people. Everyone back home thought a great deal of them both, and from what I could tell, they seemed to love their kids. It was hard to imagine his parents turning their backs on Caleb, especially after all he'd been through, but I wasn't there back then. I had no idea how bad things truly had gotten. At the same time, Caleb wasn't the same kid they kicked out all those years ago. He'd grown into a man —a good man, and I hated that they didn't know it. "You could always reach out to them...at least let them know you're alive."

"I've thought about it, but too much time has passed."

"Caleb, I've never had parents who actually gave a damn about me. They were too busy getting locked up and running out to even notice if I was alive or dead." Our eyes met as I continued, "If I had parents like yours...parents who loved me, I wouldn't let them go so easily."

"They let me go. Besides...I can't be sure that they'd even want to see me."

"You'll never know unless you try."

"Okay. You've made your point."

"Good." I smiled. "See, me being stubborn pays off from time to time."

"Um-hmm. You are something else." Caleb leaned forward and the bristles of his beard tickled my neck, causing me to quickly shy away from him. His full lips curved into a sexy smile. "Something wrong?"

"No." I giggled. "It just your beard. It tickles."

"You saying want me to shave it? 'Cause I will."

I could tell by his tone and the little spark in his eye that he was just teasing. "Don't you dare. I love your beard."

His eyes met mine in an intense gaze, and it was all I could do not to completely lose myself in him. As I lay there, looking deep into his eyes, I searched for some indication that he, too, felt this magnetic pull between us. I got my answer when he lowered his mouth down to mine, kissing me softly...so gentle and sweet. There was no better feeling than being in Caleb's arms. He made me feel safe and secure—*protected*. It was at *that* moment when I realized that my feelings for Caleb were even stronger than I thought. I was falling for him, and it terrified me. I'd learned a long time ago never to trust anyone with my heart. It had been broken too many times, and I wasn't sure I could withstand another heartbreak. But at the same time, I couldn't imagine walking away from him. I wanted Caleb too much, needed him too much, and I would do anything to have him—including putting my heart on the line.

Without removing his mouth from mine, Caleb eased on top of me, his body hovering just inches above mine as he deepened our connection. He felt so good, smelled so good, making my entire body ache for more. Overcome with the urge to touch him, my hands started to drift over his chest, gliding down over the chiseled muscles of his abdomen. I caught us both by surprise when my fingers slipped through the waistband of his boxers. A light hiss slipped through his lips when I curled my fingers around him and gently started stroking. I loved how he felt in my hand, so thick and erect, and the thought of having him inside me had me squeezing my thighs together.

Sensing my frustration, he lowered his mouth to my ear and whispered, "Tell me what you want, Darcy."

"I want you, Caleb," I answered without hesitation.

I knew he wanted to hear the words, and I gave them without any doubt in my mind. Reaching for the hem of Caleb's white t-shirt, I helped him pull it over his head. Once it was off, both our hands became frantic, quickly removing the clothes that separated us. In just a few seconds, I was lying beneath him completely bare. With his tousled, wet hair and penetrating dark eyes, Caleb was so unbelievably handsome. My heart fluttered when his hands slowly roamed over my body. "You're beautiful. Every fucking inch of you."

His hands slowly drifted up my abdomen, and a wave of lust consumed me the minute his mouth reached my breast. Hunger danced in his eyes as he looked up at me for just a brief moment, and then his mouth resumed its heavenly torture of kissing and nipping the delicate flesh. Anticipation washed over me when he settled between my thighs. His eyes met mine as he raked his cock across my clit. "Is this what you want, baby?"

"Yes." I lifted my hips, grinding against him as I tried desperately to find relief for the throbbing need that was building up inside me. "Please!"

He reached into his bedside table for a condom, and I lifted my head to watch as he slid it down his long, thick shaft. A look of satisfaction crossed his face as he settled back between my legs. He clenched his jaw before lifting my hips and driving deep inside me, filling me completely. He slowly began to move, each thrust deliberate and powerful. When I let my legs spread farther open for him, he growled, "Fuck. Never had anything feel so damn good."

"Caleb," I panted, tilting my hips towards him, wanting him deeper, harder. Sensing what I needed, he quickened his pace, as I quickly became lost in the waves of carnal sensation surrounding me and the fullness of his body inside mine. He increased his rhythm, each thrust more demanding than the last. My inner muscles clenched around him as I felt another orgasm building inside me. "Oh, God! Don't stop!"

Caleb's punishing pace never faltered as his body continued to crash into mine. I'd never felt anything like it: having him inside me was so intoxicating that I was finding it difficult to even breathe. I wanted to savor every moment...to focus on how incredible he felt, but it was all just too much. A burst of pleasure exploded inside of me, and I shuddered around him as my orgasm took over. Wrapping my legs tighter around him, I could feel the muscles in his abdomen grow taut as he finally found his own release.

We both stilled as we listened to the satisfied sounds of our hearts beating. I felt so close to him in that moment, I never wanted it to end. Eventually, our breathing began to steady, and he slowly lifted his body from mine. I wanted to wrap my arms around him and keep him close, but he'd already tossed his condom and collapsed on the bed next to me. His gaze burned into me as he brought his hand up to my neck, his fingers gently caressing my throat. "I'll never get enough of you, Darcy. Never."

"That's good, 'cause I feel the same way about you."

"I'm going to need you to be careful tomorrow morning." His expression grew serious. "'Cause I don't think I could handle it if something happened to you."

"Nothing's going to happen to me, Caleb."

I nestled myself into the crook of his arm. "I'll be careful, and besides, you and the guys will be right there watching everything that happens."

"I wish that made me feel better about all this, but it doesn't." He let out a defeated sigh. "You mean a lot to me, Darcy, more than I realized. The thought of you being in any kind of danger is..."

"Caleb, *stop*. It's going to be fine. I promise."

"I'm gonna hold you to that."

"I'm good with that." I leaned up on my elbow and looked down at him with a smile. "And in case you were wondering, you mean a lot to me too. More than I realized."

He didn't respond. Instead, he reached for the nape of my neck and pulled me towards him, and when our mouths met, he kissed me long and hard. Just as my pulse was starting to race, he pulled back and said, "You better get some sleep. You've gotta get up early."

I nodded, then curled back into my spot and closed my eyes. It seemed like I'd just dozed off when Caleb woke me to tell me it was time to get ready. I was in a sleep fog as I pulled back the covers and dragged myself into the bathroom for a shower. I was still a little groggy while I was getting dressed, but thankfully, Caleb noticed my sleepy state and brought me a cup of coffee. I was finally starting to perk up when he asked, "You ready for this?"

"As ready as I'll ever be."

He reached for my hand as he led me out of his room and down the hall. I was feeling pretty good about things until we got to Riggs's room. Clay was already there, along with Gus and a couple of the other guys. My nerves kicked into high gear the second Riggs called me over to him and started fitting me for an earpiece. His voice was calm and soothing as he said, "We'll be able to communicate back and forth with both you and Clay through these transmitters."

"I wasn't expecting you guys to be so high-tech."

"Rather be safe than sorry." As Riggs hid my mic under the collar of my shirt, he explained, "The mic is pretty sensitive. Just talk normal, and we should hear everything that's said."

"Okay."

"We don't want to rattle you, so I'll only use the earpiece if there's something you need to be aware of or if there's trouble headed your way."

"Okay."

He handed me a small, black, circular object about the size of a bottle cap and said, "Here's one of the cameras. You need to hide it the best you can without blocking the view."

"I'll do my best."

"We wouldn't be sending you in to plant these cameras if it wasn't important, but I don't want either of you taking any chances," Gus warned from behind. "Get in and get out. Understood?"

Clay and I both nodded. "Yes, sir."

Seconds later, I was following the guys out to the parking lot. Riggs went over everything one last time before giving me the cameras. I was putting them in my pocket when Caleb walked up to me. The poor guy looked like he was about to lose his lunch as he glanced down at me and said, "Remember what I said last night."

"I will."

"Just do like Riggs said. Don't take any chances."

"I won't." Seeing that worried look in his eyes was starting to get to me, so I eased up on my tiptoes and gave him a quick kiss. "I'll be back before you know it."

Before he could say anything else, I got in the car next to Clay and closed the door. Seconds later, he was pulling through the gate and driving towards downtown. I glanced back in my sideview mirror, and just like they promised, Riggs and the others were right behind us. I'd like to say that it made me feel better, but it didn't. After all the warnings and concerned looks I'd been given, I was on the brink of freaking out. I thought I was managing to keep my nervousness hidden from Clay until he asked, "You doing okay over there?"

"Yeah, I'm good."

"You wanna talk about how this is going to go down?"

"Yeah, I think that's a good idea." The first time I met Clay, I was a little intimidated by his size. He was taller than most of the guys in the club and built like a football player, but he seemed like a really good guy, always eager to give the brothers a hand whenever they needed it. While I'd often wondered why he didn't wear a cut, I knew better than to ask. I'd forgotten that the guys were listening in when I turned to Clay and suggested, "I think it would be better if you waited in the driveway while I go up to the house and ask to see KeShawn."

Startled, I flinched in my seat when I heard Riggs's voice coming through my earpiece. "Don't think that's a good idea."

"KeShawn isn't going to be happy that I'm showing up there unannounced. It doesn't make sense to make matters worse by showing up at his door with some guy, especially one the size of the fucking Hulk." I took in a breath as I gave him a moment to consider what I'd said before I added, "If he waits out by the car, hopefully KeShawn will be less suspicious, especially when it comes to getting inside the house."

"You're probably right, but—"

"You're going to have to trust me on this, Riggs."

He let out a deep breath before saying, "Fine, but if I get the slightest feeling something isn't right, I'm sending him in."

"Deal."

Moments later, Clay was pulling up in KeShawn's driveway. I sat there for a moment to check out my surroundings, and the house didn't look as bad as I thought it would. It was pretty rundown, with a dilapidated front porch and overgrown yard, but it still looked a hell of a lot better than where I grew up. Several cars were in the driveway, but there was no one outside—just an old stray sniffing around for scraps. After I unbuckled my seatbelt, I inhaled a deep breath and reached for the door handle. I figured it was best to give the guys a heads up, so I announced, "We're here, and I'm about to go to the door."

"We've got you both in sight. Just be careful and remember...don't take any chances."

"I won't." As I opened the door, I glanced over at Clay and said, "Wish me luck."

I got out, and as soon as I started towards the house, the front door opened, and two men stepped out onto the porch. I could hear my pulse pounding in my ears as I continued forward, trying to pretend like my reasons for being there were completely innocent. As I approached the porch, I gave the two men a slight smile as I asked, "Is KeShawn around?"

"Who's asking?"

"I'm Darcy Harrington. He wanted me to come by and see a Suzuki GSX-R that he wanted painted." Neither of them moved. Instead, they both just stood there staring at me with their beady little eyes. "He's expecting me to come by. Just ask him."

One of them turned and walked back inside, while the other never took his eyes off of me. I glanced back at Clay and saw that he was leaning against the driver's side door, watching as I waited for KeShawn to appear. Thankfully, I didn't have to wait long. After just a couple of minutes, KeShawn came out the front door and over towards me. "Darcy, what the hell are you doing here?"

"You told me to come by and check out the Suzuki you wanted painted."

With an aggravated grimace, he asked, "You got any idea what time it is?"

"Yeah, sorry about that." I motioned back to Clay as I said, "I stayed at my boyfriend's place night and thought I'd stop by on my way to work."

"It's not a good day for this shit. Got some stuff going on in my garage...a water leak or something." He glanced behind him before continuing, "You're gonna have to come back some other time."

"Oh, I hate to hear that." I had to think of something quick, or the plan was going to completely fall apart. "I'm not sure when I'll have a chance to get back here. Are you positive I can't take a quick look?"

"Not today. Like I told ya, it ain't a good time," he replied sounding annoyed.

"I understand. We'll get together some other time." I turned and glanced at Clay before looking back at KeShawn. "Before I go, do you mind if borrow your bathroom for a quick minute? My guy was in a rush this morning, and I didn't get a chance to take care of things."

He looked at me like I'd completely lost it as he asked, "Take care of things?"

"You know...that time of the month and all. I'd rather him not know, if you get what I'm saying."

A disgusted look crossed his face as he nodded. "Yeah, go ahead, but make it quick. Me and the boys have something we need to take care of."

"Thank you." As I started up the steps, he opened the door for me. "Where's the bathroom?"

"Down the hall on your right."

I hurried past him, and the second I entered the living

room, I took a quick glance around the room. Like the rest of the house, it was pretty run-down with old furniture that looked like it had been used and abused for years. The walls were dingy from all the smoking, and empty beer bottles and full ashtrays were scattered on the coffee table. I was just about to reach into my pocket for one of the cameras when two guys walked in. One was young, maybe in his early twenties, while the other was much older, at least fifty. They both gave me a strange look. "I was just looking for the bathroom."

The older guy pointed down the hall and said, "It's the second door on the right."

"Thanks."

I smiled as I walked past them and headed towards the bathroom. Just before I stepped inside, I noticed a small shelf in the hallway. I took a quick look around to make sure no one was watching, then reached into my pocket and took out one of the cameras. After I'd hidden it next to a picture frame, I slipped into the bathroom and closed the door. I was trying to think of a plan when I heard, "Good work on that first camera. You think you'll be able to place the others?"

"I don't know. It's going to be tough. Two guys just walked into the living room, and there might be a couple more in the kitchen, but I'll think of something."

I'd only been waiting a couple of seconds when someone banged on the door. "What's taking so long in there?"

"Sorry, I'll be right out!"

Panicked, I flushed the commode and turned on the water at the sink. After I shut it off, I was about to reach for the door when I heard someone shout, "Yo, Knuckles!"

"What?"

"You and Slade need to make a run to the sto!" the guy in the kitchen barked. "Need to grab some food for that bitch in the garage."

"Wouldn't have to feed her if we just put a goddamn bullet in her head," one of the guys in the living room grumbled in return.

"Just fucking do it, man," the man ordered. "You know Slayer will have your ass if you don't."

"Goddamn, man. I just sat down."

"Enough with your bitching and move your ass. The both of you!"

"I'm sick of this shit." I heard footsteps shuffling around in the living room, and just before they walked out, the guy yelled, "We'll be back in fifteen."

After I heard the front door slam, I waited a few more seconds to make certain they'd gone before peeking my head out into the hall. When I didn't see anyone, I hurried back to the living room and searched for a place to put the cameras. Time wasn't on my side, so I placed one on the TV stand between a couple of old books and another on the mantle. I was looking for a place to put the last camera when I heard Riggs say, "That's good, Darcy. Now, get the hell outta there."

"I'm on my way out."

When I turned around, I was shocked to see that KeShawn had entered the living room, and he was watching me. "What the fuck are you doing?"

"Umm...nothing," I answered with my voice trembling. "I was just...looking to see if they were gonna say who won the Grizzlies' game last night."

"The Grizzlies didn't play last night." The moment he took a step towards me, I knew I was screwed. I could see it in his eyes. "So, I'll ask again...What the fuck are you doing snooping around here?"

"I-I," I stammered.

"Fuck! I should've known something was up the second you showed up here this morning."

"No. Nothing's up, KeShawn." Trying desperately to convince him that he was wrong, I started, "I was just using the bathroom and—"

"You can stop with the bullshit." He stopped in front of me and crossed his arms. "I know why you're here."

"What do you mean? I told you why I was here."

"They sent you here," he barked.

"They? They who?"

"Satan's Fury." He glanced out the window as he snarled, "I'm guessing your boyfriend out there is one of them too. *Piece of shit*. I can't wait to put a fucking bullet in his head."

"No, you've got it all wrong. He's not one of them. Neither of us has anything to do with Satan's Fury!" I cried. "I came here because you asked me to. You told me to come by and see your bike, so—"

"Enough. I don't want to hear any more." He shook his head with an aggravated growl. "They *really don't know* who they're fucking with, but they're about to find out."

He grabbed me by the arm and started to drag me out of the living room towards the kitchen. As we passed a couple of his men, he looked to them and said, "Call the others. Tell them to get their asses over here now! We've got company coming."

Before they could respond, he pulled me through the back door and into the garage. Knowing Riggs and the others were listening, I tried to pull free from KeShawn's grasp as I asked, "What the hell is going on with you? Why are you bringing me to the garage?"

"Coming here was a mistake, Darcy. A big fucking mistake." He yanked me over to a door in the back of the garage, then reached into his pocket and pulled out a key. As soon as he'd unlocked the door, he gave me a hard shove, and my heart dropped the moment I spotted Kenadee bound to a chair in the middle of the room. Her face was bruised and there was blood on her clothes, but she was alive. She tried to speak but couldn't with the duct tape covering her mouth.

Trying to keep up with my act, I looked over to KeShawn and asked, "Who is that? Why do you have her tied up like that?"

Without answering, he took his fist and slammed it into my stomach, forcing the air to rush from my lungs. "I told you. I don't believe a fucking word out of your mouth, so stop with your bullshit!"

I was gasping for air and hadn't even noticed he'd taken some rope from the back wall. He yanked my arms behind me and quickly tied them together, then pushing me back, he forced me down into a chair and tied my ankles. Once he was certain I couldn't move, he walked over to Kenadee and grabbed a fistful of her hair as he turned to me and snarled, "I can't believe you came here for her! The fucking whore who let my boy die?"

"Please, stop. Just let us go!"

He didn't. Instead, he took a switch blade from his back pocket. My eyes were immediately drawn to the long, sharp blade that he pointed in my direction as he spoke, "You know, he only had two bullet wounds...one in the shoulder and one in the gut. No reason for him to bleed out like he did, but this bitch wouldn't help him. She thought he was just some piece of trash off the street who didn't deserve to live, so she just let him bleed out."

Tears streamed down Kenadee's face as she shook her head no, pleading incoherently against the tape that covered her mouth. Sadly, KeShawn paid her no mind. Instead, he took the knife and jabbed it into her left shoulder, causing her face to contort into a pained grimace as her muffled screams echoed through the room. I couldn't believe my eyes. He'd actually stabbed her, and there wasn't a damn thing I could do to stop him. He left the knife protruding from her shoulder; blood stained her pink t-shirt as it trickled down her side. I was still in complete shock, unable to even speak, when he took out a second knife and started towards her again. Horrified, I jerked at my restraints, trying to break free, and screamed, "Don't! Stop!"

My pleas were all in vain. He'd already driven the second knife into her stomach. Kenadee's tear-soaked eyes fixed on me in anguish as she slowly started to lose consciousness.

"Now, you get to feel what my boy felt...you get to bleed out nice and slow." He turned his attention to me as he snarled, "You enjoy watching your little friend bleed to death while I go kill your boyfriend and all his brothers."

With that, he turned and walked out of the room, locking the door behind him. I looked over to Kenadee, and it was like something out of a horror movie when I saw those knives sticking out of her. Knowing I had to do something before she bled to death, I searched the room for something that could help free me from my restraints, but there was nothing to be found. I was starting to freak out when I heard, "Darcy?"

"Riggs!"

"We're here with you," he said calmly. "We heard everything."

"Kenadee…h-he…stabbed her…*twice*." I was trembling all over. "It's bad—really, really bad."

"We know, and we're coming. Just hold on."

"Clay! He said he's going—"

"Heard that too. We've got him." Riggs sounded so unmoved, so rational as he said, "Now, just try to remain calm, and we'll get to you both as soon as we can."

Rider

I was about to lose it. My worst fears had come true, and it was killing me that I couldn't do anything about it. We were parked at an abandoned gas station, just two blocks from the house, but it felt like we were a million miles away. I wanted to get out of that fucking SUV and charge into Lewis's place, kill every one of those motherfuckers, but that wasn't an option. We couldn't move until Gus gave the word and that wasn't going to happen until he and the rest of the brothers arrived. I had no choice but to remain in the SUV alongside Riggs, Blaze, and Murphy and listen helplessly as Lewis dragged Darcy into that garage. I knew right then that things were about to get bad. I just didn't know how bad. We all sat silently as we listened to Lewis's every word, and it gutted us all when Kenadee's pain-stricken screams echoed through Darcy's earpiece. There was no questioning whether or not he'd hurt her. We knew he had, which meant we had to get to them both as quickly as we could. That only made the waiting that much harder. My gut twisted into a knot as I listened to Darcy plead, "Okay...Please hurry."

"We're coming," Riggs promised. "Just hold tight."

As soon as he got off the radio with Darcy, Blaze lost it. "He fucking stabbed her—we've gotta fucking do something, now!"

"Gus and the others are coming, brother," Riggs reminded him. "It won't be much longer."

"I'll fucking kill that motherfucker. I'm going to rip him limb from limb for putting his hands on her."

None of us were surprised by Blaze's reaction. We all knew how much he loved Kenadee, and knowing that he couldn't get to her right away was eating away at him. Hell, it was getting to us all. The whole thing was fucked up, and I hated that Darcy was caught right in the middle of it all. I hated even more that she wouldn't have been there if it hadn't been for us. We'd put her in harm's way, and I'd never be able to forgive myself for that. The thought of something happening to Darcy made me regret not being completely honest with her the night before. I'd told her that I cared about her, but the truth was I'd fallen for her. Hell, even that was putting it lightly. I loved her, and I wanted to make her mine in every way, and now her life was in danger. I might have made a mistake by letting her help us like she did, but I refused to lose her because of it. I would get her out of there, safe and sound, and not only that—I, along with my brothers, would end KeShawn Lewis and the rest of the Disciples once and for all.

I wasn't the only one who was set on taking them down. Murphy made his desire known the second he told Blaze, "We'll get them all. Every last one of them."

"Damn straight. I can't wait to get my hands on that motherfucker."

Murphy leaned over to Riggs and asked, "What about Clay? Where is he now?"

A couple of Disciples came out of the house shooting. Clay shot back a couple of rounds and killed one of them before we had a chance to tell him to get the hell out of there. Since then, we hadn't heard a word from him. "I don't know. I told him to head back to the clubhouse."

Eager to get things rolling, I looked over to him and asked, "Are we set to move as soon as Gus and the others get here?"

"Yeah, but Lewis called in the rest of his crew." Riggs turned the laptop so we could see the screen. "I'm just checking the cameras Darcy hid, and it looks like they're starting to roll in."

We leaned forward, and in a matter of minutes, the number of men in the house had more than tripled; they were already positioned at each entrance and all the windows with one or more AR-15 style semi-automatic rifles prepared to fire. Fuck. Concerned, I turned to Murphy and said, "Those fuckers are everywhere. How the fuck are we supposed to get close enough to the house to even get to them?"

"We'll figure something out."

"I don't see how. Looks like they've got the upper hand," I grumbled. "They're in that house, armed and hidden, and here we sit...the middle of *broad fucking daylight* and not so much as a bush for fucking cover."

I'd barely gotten the words out of my mouth when Gus and the rest of the brothers pulled up next to us. I was surprised to see that Gus wasn't in one of the SUVs with the others though. Instead, he was driving an old pickup truck that had been sitting at the garage for months. It wasn't until he opened the door to get out that I noticed that the front seat was full of explosives with several more in the back. He came over to the driver's side window and asked, "What's the latest on the girls?"

"They're both still locked up in that fucking garage," Riggs answered. "Darcy's trying to hold it together, but it's hard to tell with Kenadee. I got a feeling it's bad—*really bad*."

"We need to get in there, now. Any idea what we're dealing with on the inside?"

"They're set up and waiting. They've barricaded themselves up in the house with every window and entrance covered."

"Figured as much." Gus motioned his hand towards the old truck. "I've got us covered."

Riggs looked over into the truck, and as if he'd just read Gus's mind, he nodded and said, "I like your way of thinking, Prez."

"I thought you might." Sounding hopeful, Gus asked him, "You think you can get these rigged up in time?"

"Shouldn't take long." Riggs handed Blaze his laptop as he said, "Keep an eye on things. Let me know if anything changes."

Murphy and I followed as Riggs got out and headed over to the pickup truck. We helped him start wiring them together while the others started prepping to go to war with the Disciples. As soon as Riggs had the detonator set up, he went over to get his laptop from Murphy. Once he'd confirmed that everything was ready to go, he looked to Gus and said, "Looks like we're all set."

"Good. Now, we just have to decide on the best location for the hit."

"I'd say the living room is the ideal spot," Murphy answered. "There's at least ten of them positioned there, and it can be accessed from the main road."

"I agree." Riggs also added, "And it's far enough from the garage that we don't have to worry about it being too close to the girls."

"Okay. Now, we just have to decide who's going to drive."

Shadow was the first to step forward and say, "I'll do it."

"No, brother." Blaze turned to Riggs as he asked, "Where do you want it?"

Riggs pulled up an image of the house, and as he pointed to the left corner, he told him, "I would say right here is your best option. That way you won't have to worry about clearing the front porch steps, but there is the issue of the side windows."

"They'll start shooting the second they see me coming their way."

"Exactly."

"Don't give a fuck," Blaze snarled. "I'll make it happen."

"I know you will," Gus replied before turning to the rest of us. "We're going to have to move fast on this. We gotta get in and out before the cops have a chance to show. We don't want anyone identifying us, so remove your cuts and keep your heads low."

As soon as we were ready, Blaze got behind the wheel of the truck, and we all watched as he pulled out of the parking lot. The second he was on the main road, he slammed his foot on the accelerator, and with us following close behind, he sped towards Lewis's place. Just as we'd expected, the minute Blaze got close, the Disciple's started shooting, doing everything they could to stop him, but it simply wasn't enough. Blaze just kept plowing towards them, and with the house situated on a corner lot, he was able to reach enough speed to cause some real damage to it. When he was just a few feet away, he opened the door and jumped out, hitting the ground just before the truck crashed through the side of the structure. Riggs immediately hit the detonator, and an explosion like none other erupted through the house. While the Disciples were scrambling to get away from the heat of the fire, we made our move, charging towards the building while shooting anyone who came stumbling out.

In a matter of minutes, it was clear that we'd taken control of the situation. The shooting slowed, and there was little activity happening inside the house. When the brothers started to span out, I veered to the left and made my way to the garage. I had to get to Darcy, see that she was okay before I lost my mind. As I rounded the corner, I came face to face with the devil himself—KeShawn Lewis. I had my Glock drawn, aimed right at his head, but he was equally prepared and had the barrel of his AR-15 directed right at me. "You guys think you got the best of me, but it's gonna take more than some stunt like that to take me down!"

"It's time to face the music, asshole. You're never gonna get out of here alive. You're done!"

"That's what you think," he scoffed. "I'm just gettin' started!"

"Really? And what exactly do you think you're gonna do? Most, if not all, of your crew is dead." I looked him straight in the eye. "You gonna take on Fury by yourself?"

"Don't gotta take you all on. Right now, I just gotta get through you"—he motioned his head towards the weapon he had pointed in my direction—"and from where I stand, it looks like I shouldn't have any problem doing that."

I was beginning to think he might be right, but then,

out of the corner my eye, I noticed movement from behind the garage. Seconds later, Clay came into view. He gave me a slight nod, and I knew I had to keep KeShawn distracted. "You never should've taken the girl, and you sure as hell shouldn't have hurt her."

"How the fuck you know I hurt her?" His eyes narrowed for a moment, and then he grumbled. "*Darcy*...I knew that bitch was here because of you. I should've put a bullet in her head the second I found her snooping around my house."

When Clay stepped up behind, I knew it was over. I waited as he raised his gun up to KeShawn's head, then I said, "Like I told you before, you'll never get out of here alive."

Clay pressed the barrel of his gun against KeShawn's head and said, "Drop it asshole!"

"You might as well pull the trigger 'cause that ain't never gonna happen, you piece of shit sonofabitch."

Lewis stood there glaring at me with an angry scowl marking his face, refusing to move. Clay started to squeeze his trigger when a shot was fired behind me. Lewis shifted in his step, wincing as he quickly lowered his AR and placed his free hand on his thigh. "Goddamn it!"

I looked over to see who'd taken the shot and spotted Blaze standing a few yards away with his gun still trained on KeShawn. He'd just started towards us with a fierce look in his eyes. As soon as he got over to us, he looked to Clay and asked, "What the fuck are you still doing here?"

"I know I was supposed to go back to the clubhouse, but I couldn't leave. Not like that." Clay looked down at Lewis as he snarled, "Not when this fucking asshole had taken Darcy."

"When you're given an order ..."

Blaze's voice trailed off as his attention was suddenly drawn to something behind me. His eyes suddenly widened, and all the blood drained from his face. Curious to see what had him so rattled, I turned around and found Darcy trying to support Kenadee as they stumbled out of the garage. While Darcy seemed to be okay, Kenadee looked like she was barely hanging on. Relief washed over her face when she looked up and saw Blaze and me rushing towards them. As soon as he approached, Darcy passed Kenadee off to Blaze, and as he lowered her to the ground, he shouted, "Oh, God. What the hell did he do to you!"

"She wouldn't let me take the knives out," Darcy cried. "She said she'd bleed out and die if I did."

"She's right. You did the right thing leaving them," I told her.

"I need you to hold on, Kenadee," Blaze pleaded. "Do you hear me?"

I could still hear gunshots going off behind us as Darcy warned, "I don't think she can hang on much longer. We've got to get her to the hospital."

With his gun still trained on KeShawn, Clay turned to us and said, "My car is right around back."

"Okay, let's get her to his car." Blaze looked down at Kenadee as he told her, "Hang on, baby. We're getting you to the hospital."

Kenadee shook her head as she said, "No. You can't take me...Someone might connect the club to all this. You have to let Darcy take me. It's the only way."

"I'm not leaving you, Kenadee."

"You don't have a choice. Too many questions."

"As much as I hate to say it, she's right, brother. It's best to let Clay take her."

"Fuck."

Kenadee placed the palm of her hand on Blaze's cheek. "I'll be okay. Right now, I need you to finish. I want it to be over."

"I'll be there as soon as I can." Blaze motioned for Clay to come help with Kenadee, and once we had her up on her feet, he ordered, "Call me the second you get her to the hospital."

Clay nodded, then he and Darcy rushed her to his car. Once they had Kenadee safely secured inside, they took off towards the hospital. As soon as they were gone, Blaze turned to me and said, "I've got him. You go check on the others and see if they need a hand."

After seeing the state Kenadee was in, it was no surprise that Blaze wanted to deal with Lewis on his own. Understanding what it meant to him, I nodded. "I'll be waiting for you around front."

As I started to walk away, I could hear Blaze talking to Lewis, but I couldn't make out exactly what he was saying. It didn't matter. Lewis's end was coming, and knowing Blaze the way I did, I knew it wouldn't be pretty. I'd just rounded the corner when Murphy and several of the others came rushing towards me. I was giving them a quick rundown of what had transpired with Kenadee and Darcy when I heard a round of gunshots coming from the back of the house. I knew then it was over. The only remaining Disciple had met his end.

Darcy

When I came out of the garage and saw that Caleb was there, I wanted to rush over and wrap my arms around him, but I couldn't. I knew if I did, that tiny shred of strength I was clinging to would break, and I'd completely fall apart. I couldn't let that happen. I had to keep it together until we got Kenadee the help she needed. I'd managed to keep my wits about me as Clay raced us over to the hospital. I was even able to get Kenadee inside and admitted without sounding like a deranged lunatic, but the minute the doctors carried her away on that gurney, the dam started to crack. I fought to hold back the tears, but it wasn't easy, especially when Caleb came walking into the waiting room. The moment he started towards me with that intense look in his eyes, I couldn't hold on any longer. The tears started to fall as he brought me into his arms. I felt so safe in his arms, and it wasn't long before tension and fear started to fade, and I felt like I could breathe again. He was still holding me close to his chest as he whispered, "I'm right here. I've got you."

"I was scared...KeShawn was so angry." My voice trembled as I told him, "He wouldn't listen to me."

His voice was filled with anguish as he murmured, "I should've never let you go in there like that."

"No one asked me to go. Not you or your brothers." I stepped back and looked up at him. "I volunteered. I knew the risk I was taking."

"Doesn't matter. It's my job to keep you safe."

"Your job?" I scoffed. "What's that supposed to mean?"

He lifted his hand up to my face, gently running the pad of his thumb across my cheek. "Because you're mine, Darcy, and it's my job to protect what's mine. I failed at that today, but I give you my word, I'll never let it happen again."

While his words meant everything to me, it was the way he said them with such emotion and intensity that made me realize I'd finally found him—the man I could truly trust with my heart. Unable to speak, I wrapped my arms around Caleb and pulled him close. I was still holding on to him when Blaze walked in with the rest of the brothers following close behind. As soon as they spotted us, Blaze rushed over and asked, "Has there been any word on Kenadee?"

"They took her up to surgery about twenty minutes ago."

There was no missing the worry in his voice as he asked, "Did they say anything else...like how she was doing or how long the surgery would take?"

"I wish I knew more, but since I wasn't family, they wouldn't tell me anything."

I'd barely gotten the words out of my mouth when a beautiful blonde nurse walked in. The minute she spotted Blaze, she rushed over to him and said, "I just heard that they took Kenadee up to surgery. What the hell happened?"

"I can't get into that right now, Robyn."

"Of course, you can't," she complained. "Can you at least tell me how she's doing?"

"I would if I knew."

"Well, damn. You'd think they'd come tell her husband what the hell was going on," she said and huffed. "Give me a minute, and I'll go see what I can find out."

"Thanks, Robyn."

When she turned to walk away, Caleb leaned over to me and said, "Robyn is one of Kenadee's best friends. They work together, and even lived together before Kenadee and Blaze hooked up."

"Hopefully, she'll be able to find out something."

"Oh, she will. Robyn always finds a way to get what she wants."

Turns out that Caleb was right. It wasn't long before Robyn returned to the waiting room, and from the look on her face, I was worried that she didn't have good news to share. When she started towards us, Blaze stood up and asked, "Did you find out anything?"

"Yeah, I was able to talk to one of the nurses in the operating room with Kenadee." She wrung her hands, twisting them nervously as she spoke. "Dr. Foust is the surgeon working on her, and that's really good because he's the very best."

"Okay, what else?"

"The knife in her abdomen nicked her spleen, but the damage was minimal. Right now, it looks like she's holding her own. Stats are good, and they've got her blood count back up."

Even though I didn't know Robyn, I could tell that

something was worrying her, and I wasn't the only one who'd noticed. Blaze clearly picked up on it too. He took a step towards her as he asked, "Why do I get the feeling there's something you aren't telling me?"

"The important thing to remember is that she's going to pull through this."

"Dammit, Robyn! Just tell me what's going on!"

"She's pregnant, Blaze. Looks to be about ten or eleven weeks along," Robyn finally admitted.

"Pregnant? She never told me anything about being pregnant."

"I don't think she knew. If she did, she would've told me, and she sure as hell would've told you." Robyn placed her hand on Blaze's shoulder. "There's a good chance the baby will be okay."

"When will we know for sure?"

"It's hard to tell. It'll take some time to see if the anesthesia has any adverse effects." Trying to be optimistic, she continued, "Right now, we need to focus on the fact that Kenadee is doing okay. We have to make sure she pulls through this, and then we'll worry about the other, okay?"

"How much longer before she gets out of surgery?"

"It shouldn't be much longer. I'm going to head upstairs, so I can be there when they take her into recovery." She gave him a quick hug before she turned to leave. "I'll call you the minute I know something."

"Thanks, Robyn."

Once she left the room, we went over and sat down with Blaze, waiting silently to hear something back from Robyn. The adrenaline that was pumping through my body was starting to fade, making me suddenly feel like I'd been hit by a truck. Noting my fatigue, Caleb slipped his arm around my shoulder, and I rested my head on his chest, quietly watching as Blaze got up and started pacing around the waiting room. It was impossible not to feel sorry for him as he returned to his seat and dropped his head into the palms of his hands. The man was really struggling, but his spirits seemed to lighten when his parents walked in with his son, Kevin. As expected, they had a million questions, and Blaze tried to answer them the best he could. A troubled expression marked Kevin's face as he listened to his father describe Kenadee's condition, but he kept his concerns to himself as he sat down next to Blaze, quietly trying to give his father the support he needed. While it had to be difficult for Blaze to sit there not knowing what was going on with Kenadee, it was clear that having his son close was helping him a great deal.

It had been over an hour since Robyn had left to go upstairs, and there still hadn't been any word from her. We were all getting anxious to hear something and were relieved when Blaze's burner started to ring. We watched as he answered the call, each studying his reaction to see if it was good news or bad, and we all felt a sigh of relief when a smile spread across his face. "That's great. I'll be here waiting."

As soon as he hung up the phone, he turned to us and said, "She's out of surgery. The doctor said it went well."

"That's great news, brother," Gus told him. "When will you be able to go up and see her?"

"They're sending a nurse down now to get me."

"Great. Be sure to tell her we're here and thinking about her."

"You know I will."

Moments later, a nurse came to the waiting room and led Blaze upstairs to see Kenadee. As we sat there waiting for him to return, I looked around the room at all the brothers. Not a single one of them looked like they were restless or eager to leave. They weren't there out of some unspoken obligation. They were there because they truly wanted to be. Having support like that wasn't something I was accustomed to. In fact, I'd never really had anyone who was there for me. I always had to look out for myself—not that I'd ever really had a choice in the matter. But things were changing. Now, I didn't have to be on my own anymore. The thought had me leaning towards Caleb. As I rested my head on his chest, he ran his hand down my back and said, "You never told me how you managed to get out of the garage with Kenadee."

"I got lucky, I guess." I lifted my head and looked up at Caleb as I told him, "KeShawn was so angry when he thought I was snooping around his place, even more so when he realized I was there for the club. I guess that's why he didn't tie me up tight enough."

"So, you were able to pull free on your own?"

"Yeah, with a little work. Once I'd untied myself, I went over and did the same for Kenadee. I couldn't believe how calm she was during the whole thing, especially when she told me about not removing the knives. I can't tell you how hard it was to see her like that. I knew I had to get her out of there, but I had no idea how I was going to do it until I heard that explosion." Just thinking about the sound of the explosion and the screams that followed sent a chill down my spine. "I had no idea what was going on when I heard all the screaming and gunshots but hoped that Lewis and his men would be distracted enough for us to get away. I used an old paperclip to pick the lock."

"You're really something. You know that, right?"

"Why? Because I let KeShawn catch me in his living room and lock me in garage?" I scoffed.

"Because you kept your shit together and managed to get not only yourself, but Kenadee, out of that garage alive."

"That's only because you showed up when you did." I laid my head back down on his chest. "Thank you for that, by the way. I can't tell you how relieved I was to see you."

Before he could respond, Blaze walked back into the waiting room looking completely different than he had when he left. The tension was gone from his shoulders, and he was almost smiling. The entire room fell silent as he walked over to us and said, "Things are looking good. Kenadee is still pretty out of it, but her stats are looking good and she's talking."

"That's great, brother," Gus told him.

All the guys got up and hugged him, telling him how happy they were that Kenadee was going to be okay. Once they were done, Blaze turned to them and said, "I appreciate you all coming and staying like this, but I've got it from here. Besides, I know there are things that need to be dealt with."

"We'll get gone, but you call us if anything changes," Gus replied.

"I will."

When the guys started to disperse, Caleb went over to Blaze and gave him one last hug, telling him to call if he needed anything. As soon as they were done talking, he reached for my hand and we started towards the door. We hadn't gotten far when Blaze called out to me, "Darcy, you got a minute?"

"Sure."

A serious expression crossed his face as he came over

to me and said, "I wanted to thank you for everything you did today."

"There's no need to thank me, Blaze. Especially after things turned out like they did."

"You're kidding, right? If you hadn't gotten those cameras out..." He stopped himself before he said too much. "Let's just say it would've been a hell of a lot worse."

"I'm glad I was able to help a little."

"No, Darcy. You helped a lot." His expression softened as he let out a sigh. "Because of you, Kenadee and, God willing, the baby she's carrying, are going to pull through this, and I can't thank you enough for that."

"You're very welcome, Blaze." I reached out and gave him a quick hug. "You take care of them, and please tell Kenadee to call if she needs anything."

"Will do."

Caleb led us out to the SUV where Gunner and Murphy were waiting on us, and as soon as we got in, Gunner drove us back over to the clubhouse. He had to go meet with his brothers and make sure there were no loose ends that needed tying up, so I told him I'd wait in his room until he was done. I had every intention of doing exactly what I told him, but then I remembered that I hadn't been home to feed Lenny and Scout. Knowing that they had to be hungry, I sent Caleb a text to let him know that I was running home. Instead of waiting for a response, I headed out to my truck and went on my way.

Rider

As soon as we got to the conference room, Riggs pulled up all the police scanners and reports to see if we could find anything that showed that they'd suspected our involvement in the attack against the Disciples. He took his time and went through every piece of information they'd collected, but there was no connection to Satan's Fury to be found. It seemed that the cops were solely focused on the Red Knights. Since the Knights were known rivals of the Disciples and most of their members had suddenly come up missing, they assumed that the attack was some sort of retaliation. Gus, along with the rest of us, was pleased to hear that we were in the clear. I thought he was about to dismiss us when Murphy turned to him and asked, "Any updates on Dane or Gauge?"

"I checked in with Mack earlier, and he said Dane's improving. He should make a full recovery." A half-smile crossed Gus's face as he continued, "And we all know how Gauge can be. He's too stubborn to let a couple of gunshot wounds slow him down."

"Good to hear," Murphy replied. "And what about

Clay? Have you made any decisions about him prospecting?"

"I was having my doubts about him until today," Gus replied. "Blaze said that he really stepped up to the plate."

"He did," I replied. "Saved my ass, that's for sure."

"Really? How's that?"

"I was on the way to the garage to see about Kenadee and Darcy when I came face to face with Lewis and his AR-15. We were in the middle of a standoff and it wasn't looking good for me when Clay came out of nowhere. He came up behind him, put his gun to Lewis's head, and was able to distract him long enough for Blaze to take a shot. I don't want to think about what might've happened if he hadn't shown up when he did," I explained.

"Sounds like he did good."

"He did, and don't forget, he was also the one who got Kenadee and Darcy to the hospital. Having his car close came in handy."

"I remember." Gus thought for a moment, then said, "I also remember that Riggs told him to get his ass back to the clubhouse. He didn't follow orders."

"I get that. I also get that he didn't want to leave without Darcy," I replied. "I think it shows that he's finally starting to get the meaning of brotherhood."

"I hope you're right." Gus ran his hand down his beard as he thought for a moment, then said, "You've all been around Clay, and I'm sure you all have your own opinions about him. I'd say it's time for us to make a decision. Are we going to let him prospect or are we going to send him back to Viper?"

"He's got a lot to learn, but honestly, I think Rider's right. This kid's got something," Shadow replied. "I'd say give him a try."

Murphy nodded. "I agree. Once he builds some confidence in himself and learns the ropes, I think he'll be an asset to the club."

"He's got my vote," I added.

"Are we all in agreement?" When the rest of the brothers gave their consent, Gus announced, "Then, it's settled. We'll let Clay prospect, and hopefully, he'll do us proud."

As soon as we were dismissed, I went back to my room to find Darcy. When I opened the door, I was surprised to see that she wasn't there. Worried that something might be wrong, I reached into my pocket for my phone. I was about to dial her number when I saw that I had a text message from her saying that she was headed home. Even though I knew Lewis was dead, I still didn't like the idea of her going to her house alone. I quickly dialed her number, but she didn't answer. That didn't set too well for me, so I grabbed my keys and headed out to my bike. After everything that had happened at Lewis's place and the hospital, I'd let my panic take hold, and my imagination started to run wild as I sped over to Darcy's. By the time I made it to her place, I was a fucking wreck. I got off my bike, and was racing up her steps when I heard, "Well, lookie there. The handsome, young biker is back!"

I glanced over and found Thelma and Louise sitting on their porch with blankets thrown across their knees and a cup of what I thought was coffee in their hands. "Hi, ladies. How you making it today?"

"We're doing just fine," the lady with the purple tinted hair answered. "It's so nice to see you again."

"Good to see you too."

"Would you care to join us for a hot toddy?" she

offered. "Frances has outdone herself with these. They sure hit the spot."

"I appreciate the offer, but I need to get in here and see about Darcy."

"We were sure glad to see her this afternoon. We were worried about her."

"Oh, yeah?"

"Absolutely. It's not like her not to come home, especially for two nights in a row," the other lady replied. "We were beginning to think you'd stolen her away from us. Isn't that right, Alice?"

"That's right."

"I'm sorry we had you worried."

"No need to apologize, dear." She took a sip of her toddy before she said, "Just so you know, we aren't just a couple of nosey biddies poking into Darcy's business. It's not that at all. We think a lot of that sweet girl, and it's hard not to worry about her. That's all."

"I understand. I think a lot of her too."

"Well, that's really good to hear. I hope that means you can appreciate just how wonderful she is."

"I do."

"Well, if you happen to forget, Alice and I will be sure to remind you."

"I'm sure you will." Eager to get inside to see Darcy, I continued towards the door. "You two enjoy your toddies."

"We will! Don't you worry about that."

I knocked on the door and waited, but she didn't answer. That uneasy feeling I'd felt earlier came creeping back, and I found myself reaching for the doorknob. When I found that it was unlocked, I opened the door and stepped inside. "Darcy?"

Still no answer. There was no sign of her in the living room, so I went to check her bedroom. The weight of all the tension I'd been carrying with me quickly vanished when I found her curled up on the bed, sleeping next to her cat. It was difficult to be angry with her when she looked so damn beautiful lying there. Her hair was wrapped up in a towel, and she was only wearing a long-sleeved t-shirt with a pair of over-sized socks. As I stood there staring at her, I felt a sudden need to be close to her, so I took off my cut and boots, then slowly eased into the bed next to her. When I slipped my arm around her, she nestled her back against my chest and whispered, "I thought you were meeting with the guys."

"I was." I lowered my mouth to her ear as I said, "I thought you were going to wait for me in my room."

"I was." She remained completely still with her eyes closed. "Then, I remembered I needed to get home to feed Scout and Lenny."

"And you couldn't wait for me?"

"I didn't know how long you'd be."

I could feel myself becoming frustrated as I said, "You could've asked."

"I tried. You didn't respond to my text."

"So, you waited on my response or did you just leave without really telling anyone where you were going?"

Finally catching on that I wasn't pleased with her actions, she rolled over to face me. The towel fell loose from her head, leaving her damp hair falling around her shoulders as she sassed, "I didn't realize that I needed to check in with a babysitter before I went home to feed my cat."

"Do I need to remind you what went down this morning?"

"No," she clipped. "I was there. I remember it all quite well. *Thank you.*"

"You remember, and yet you still came here alone."

"Why don't you quit beating around the bush and just say what you have to say, Caleb?"

"You know I don't like you being out here all alone." I eased up on my elbow as I looked down at her. "So, after everything that happened today, you had to know that coming here alone wouldn't set well with me. That's why you didn't wait for my response."

"I didn't wait for your response because I knew you were busy meeting with the brothers."

"That's bullshit, and you know it."

"I'm a big girl, Caleb. I can take care of myself."

I glared down at her as I growled, "Would you have been able *to take care of yourself* if one of those Disciples had gotten away from us, and he was sitting here waiting for you?"

"But there wasn't anyone here, Caleb. I'm fine."

"I get that you're used to being on your own. Hell, you've been doing it since you were just a kid, but you don't have to keep doing everything on your own anymore."

She looked up at the ceiling, and a tear trickled from the corner of her eye as she whispered, "I get what you're saying, but I'm just not used to having someone who actually cares about me and what I'm doing."

"Well, you do now, so get used to it."

"I'm trying."

I wiped a tear from her cheek. "Try harder."

"Are you always this bossy?"

"Only when it comes to something I care about."

I eased up on the bed, and never took my eyes off her

as I reached for the hem of her t-shirt, carefully pulling it over her head. Her brows furrowed as she placed her hand on my chest and said, "Wait...Do I need to be worried about one of those Disciple guys showing up here?"

"I'd say the chances of that happening are very slim."

"Then, why'd you come in here so riled up about me coming home alone?" she pushed.

"I said the chances were slim, Darcy. I didn't say it couldn't happen."

"But more or less, this thing is over, and we don't have to worry about them anymore?"

"It looks that way." I lowered my mouth to her neck and trailed kisses down her shoulder. "But it will take some time before we know for sure."

"And the police? What about them? Should I be worried about them knocking at my—"

"You don't have to worry about the cops, babe." As I hovered over her, I looked into her worried eyes as I tried to assure her, "We've got them covered. You don't have to worry about anything. I'm not going to let anything happen to you."

I watched as her beautiful, full lips curled into a mischievous smile. "Does that mean you're done being mad at me?"

"That depends." I slid my hands under her and reached for her lace panties, easing them down her long, sexy legs. "Are you going to let me in...let me take care of you and love you?"

"I told you...I'm *trying*."

I lowered my head between her legs, and with my mouth just inches from her, I demanded, "Try harder."

I brushed my tongue against her and watched as her back arched off the bed. Her soft whimpers echoed around me as I began to tease her with my mouth. When she started to squirm beneath me, I placed my hands on her thighs, holding her in place. Her taste had my cock throbbing with an uncontrollable need to be inside her, and when I couldn't wait any longer, I stood and removed my clothes. She was still in a haze, sprawled across her bed, and I couldn't take my eyes off her as I slipped on a condom. Damn. She looked so fucking beautiful as I settled between her legs. I leaned forward, placing my mouth close to her ear as I whispered, "You're mine, Darcy Harrington. Every fucking inch of you."

"And you're mine, Caleb Hughes." A sexy smirk crossed her face as she wrapped her legs around my hips and urged me forward. "Every inch of you. Now, come here and finish what you started."

Her smirk turned into a devilish grin as she shifted her hips, forcing me deeper. Unable to resist, I thrust further until I filled her completely. This woman had me completely spellbound. She'd invaded my dreams, my thoughts, and I was always left wanting more. I doubted it was possible for me to ever get enough of her. The sounds of our bodies crashing together filled the room, urging me on.

"Yes! Don't stop," she moaned as my pace gradually increased, becoming steady and unforgiving. My eyes roamed over her, taking in every inch of her gorgeous body. She was everything I'd ever wanted and more. Her chest rose and fell as she tried to steady her breath, and I growled with satisfaction when I felt her body tightening around me. Knowing she was getting close, I continued to drive inside her, over and over, constantly increasing the rhythm of my movements.

"Fuck!" I growled as my body demanded its release too

fucking soon. I wanted to take my time with her, but she was just too fucking tight, felt too fucking good to stop. I plunged inside of her again and again, feeling her spasm with her release. My hips collided into hers, faster, harder with every breath I took. Soft whimpers of my name echoed through the room as Darcy's body jolted and her orgasm ripped through her body. When she clamped down around me, I couldn't hold back any longer. My grip on her hips tightened as I buried myself deep inside one last time.

With a ragged breath, I lay down beside her, quickly tossing the condom in the trash next to the bed. After several moments, I rolled over to her and said, "I don't think anyone has ever been able to get under my skin and rile me up like you do, but I have to admit...I like making up with you."

"Well, if you must know...I like making up with you too." Her expression grew serious as she whispered, "I'm sorry about earlier. I just wasn't thinking."

"I get why you did it." I glanced over at Scout, who was now on the floor glaring at me like I was encroaching on his territory. "And I'm sure they were both relieved when they saw you coming through that front door. I know Thelma and Louise were."

"Yes, they were." Darcy shook her head. "I bet they asked me a million questions about where I'd been."

"You know earlier, when you said you weren't used to having people who cared about you or what you did...that wasn't exactly true." I reached for her and pulled her close. "Hell, you have a trailer park full of people who care a great deal about you."

"Yeah, I guess you're right about that."

"But there's not a soul around who'll ever love you the way I do."

Her eyes met mine, and I could see the emotion building inside her as she whispered, "I've spent most of my life loving you, Caleb. I loved you back when we were kids, and I love you now."

Darcy looked at me with a soul-searching stare, and I have no idea who moved first, but the next thing I knew, we were connected with her mouth pressed against mine. A light moan vibrated from her throat when my hand gripped the back of her neck as I delved deeper into her mouth. She hooked a leg over mine, arching her hips towards me, and the moment her hands started slowly drifting down my chest, I was done. I had to have her once again. We spent the next few hours tangled in each other's arms, and I still wanted more. Unfortunately, we were both exhausted, and since neither of us had eaten a bite all day, we were starving. Darcy was lying in the bed with just a sheet covering her as I rolled over and said, "I'm going to go fix us something to eat."

With a playful smirk, she replied, "Good luck with that. I don't have many groceries in there."

"I'm sure I can come up with something." I eased out of bed, and after I threw on my boxers, I headed into the kitchen. I opened the fridge and found it almost bare. Other than a half-gallon of milk, a few eggs, bacon, and a can of biscuits, there was little to be found. "You weren't kidding about the groceries."

"I tried to warn you," she called from the bedroom. "There's a pizza place around the corner that delivers."

"I've got it covered."

With her cat watching my every move, I grabbed the bacon, eggs, and biscuits, and after twenty minutes of working my magic, I'd managed to pull together a pretty decent little dinner. I was making our plates when Darcy walked up behind me. As she peered over my shoulder, she smiled and said, "It looks great."

"It'll do in a pinch."

She swiped a piece of bacon off one of the plates as she said, "I think I might like having you around."

"Is that right?"

"Great make-up sex and dinner with the man I love?" she teased. "It's pretty hard to beat that."

"Baby, I'm just getting started."

Darcy

It had been just under a month since the club's encounter with the Disciples, and things at the garage were finally starting to get back to normal. The guys were back at work, talking and joking around like usual, and even Blaze had returned. He started stopping by a few days after Kenadee was released from the hospital, trying his best to balance his time between work and home, but it wasn't easy. Even though they'd only gotten positive feedback from the doctors, we could all see that he was still worried about her and their baby. Something told me that even after the baby was born happy and healthy, he'd continue to worry about them both. It was just his nature. Blaze was a man who liked to be in control, and from the looks of it, he wasn't likely to change any time soon.

He was looking over one of my invoices as he stepped into my paint room and asked, "This says you charged an extra four-fifty for the gold overlay on the Cunningham bike."

"Yeah. Is there a problem?"

"No. I just wasn't aware that you were going to hike the

price up like that," he replied with a condescending tone. "If I had been, I would've touched base with Mike to make sure he was okay with it."

"I checked in with him." Under different circumstances, I might've been aggravated by Blaze's overstep, but I knew he was just trying to stay on top of things in hopes of keeping his customers happy. "When I started the design and saw what a difference the overlay would make, I called him. Told him what I was thinking and how much it would cost, and he was cool with the upcharge."

"So, he knows about the extra four-fifty?"

"Yep," I answered. "Agreed to it before I ever started working on it."

A pleased look crossed his face as he turned and headed back to his office. "I knew hiring you was a smart thing to do."

I couldn't help but smile as I returned my focus to the project I'd been working on. I'd spent the entire morning painting bright yellow and orange flames on the hood of a cherry-red 1971 Chevy Cheyenne, and I was about to start stenciling the front fenders when Caleb stepped into the paint room. "Hey. You got plans after work?"

"Just the usual. Why?"

"I'm heading out to Oakland this afternoon."

"Why Oakland?" The words had barely left my mouth when it hit me. "Wait...Are you seriously thinking about going to see them?"

"I am."

I couldn't believe he was actually gonna do it. Caleb had been trying to convince me to move in with him for weeks. He had a two-bedroom house downtown, just a few minutes from the garage. We'd stayed there several times over the past couple of weeks, and it was a beautiful place. It was also in a great neighborhood with plenty of room for us both, but I'd been resisting. It wasn't that I didn't want to move in with him, because I did. I wanted nothing more than to start my future with him, but before that could happen, he needed to face his past. I knew it bothered him that he'd lost ties with his folks, so I made a deal with him—I'd move in with him as soon as he reached out to his parents. I felt guilty giving him an ultimatum, but deep down I knew it was something he needed to do. At the time, I thought it would take him weeks, maybe months, before he'd give in, but clearly, I was wrong. "I wasn't sure you'd go through with it."

He cocked his eyebrow and replied. "It's not like I have much choice in the matter."

"Oh," I mumbled. "So, you're only going because I said I wouldn't move in with you unless you did?"

"Why else would I go?"

"I don't know." I placed my hand on my hip and huffed. "I'd hoped you would see that it was the right thing to do."

"If that was the case, then you wouldn't have made an *ultimatum*."

"It wasn't an ultimatum, Caleb." I loved him more every day, but there were times when he could drive me to the point of insanity. "I was just negotiating with you."

"Um-hmm." His eyes narrowed, and if I didn't know him better, I would've thought he was getting angry with me. Instead, he was simply calling me out, not letting me get away with my usual antics. "That's bullshit and you know it. You knew what you were doing when you made that deal with me."

"Okay, fine. The deal's off the table." I threw my hands up in the air with all the dramatics and sarcasm I could muster. "If you don't want to go, then don't go. I don't care what you do."

His expression softened as he stepped towards me and said, "We both know you care. That's why I wanted you to go with me to see my folks."

"Go with you?" The thought caught me by surprise. Caleb and I grew up in two different worlds, but I had no doubt that his parents knew exactly who I was. Hell, everyone in town knew about those poor Harrington kids. I knew that his first visit home would be difficult, and I didn't want to make it worse by being there. "I don't think that's such a good idea."

Pretending like he had no idea what I was talking about, he asked, "Why not?"

"Because your parents know me. They know everything about me."

"I don't give a fuck." He placed his hand on my cheek and whispered, "I'm proud to say that you're mine."

"Something tells me your parents won't feel the same."

"You are beautiful, unbelievably smart, and out-of-this-world talented, and not only that, you've got a heart of gold. If my folks can't see that I have a hotshot girlfriend, then that's their fucking loss."

"But they—"

"I'm not going unless you go with me, babe, so there's no sense in being stubborn about this," he cut me off. "You're going."

"Fine, I'll go."

Caleb leaned forward and gave me a quick kiss before saying, "Now, that's my kind of negotiating."

"Why? Because you got your way?"

"Absolutely." He snickered as he popped me on the ass. "We'll leave right after work, so be ready, hotshot."

"Hold up! Wait a cotton-pickin' minute!" T-Bone started charging in our direction as he demanded, "Tell me I didn't just hear that!"

"Hear *what?*"

"You just called her babe, brother...and hotshot after that! What the hell is that all about?" I had a feeling he wasn't being completely serious about his whole scorned act, but I had to give it to him. He was pretty damn convincing. "Here at the garage? *Seriously?*"

"What the fuck are you talking about, brother?"

"You know damn well what I'm talking about!" He huffed. "I took an ass chewing just because I called her doll."

"And?" Caleb answered like it was no big deal.

"And that shit ain't right," T-Bone pouted like a kid. "You just did the same damn thing."

"So." Making no apologies, Caleb declared, "She's my ol' lady."

"Not here, she's not. That ol' lady shit don't fly while we're at the garage," T-Bone fussed. "I've done right. I played by the rules and treated her like one of us. We all have, just like she wanted. But now, you come in and change the rules. Hell, naw. That shit ain't cool."

Caleb shrugged. "*It is what it is.*"

"Fuck that." He was putting on quite a show with his arms flailing in the air and his voice several octaves higher than normal. "What's next? You gonna start calling us 'babe' and 'hotshot' too?"

A mischievous look crossed his face as Clay stepped forward and said, "Damn, T-Bone. I didn't know your door swung that way."

Since the day Gus offered him the opportunity to prospect for the club, Clay has been doing everything he could to meet the brothers' expectations without complaint—even when he was the one they chose to do all their grunt work. It was clear that he didn't want to do anything to screw it up, so it came as a surprise to us all that he'd go head to head with T-Bone—the mouthiest brother in the club. Everyone within earshot turned to see how their brother would respond. T-Bone's face turned red and with his voice even higher than before, he spat, "What the fuck did you just say?"

"Nothing, brother," he answered mockingly. "I just never pictured you as the jealous type."

The entire garage erupted into laughter, which only pissed off T-Bone even more. "Shut the fuck up and mind your place, Prospect."

"Easy, brother." Caleb gave me a quick wink as he continued, "No need to getting riled up. There's enough of me to go around."

"Fuck you, Rider. Just...just...*fuck you*," he stammered in frustration.

I felt a little guilty that I was the reason behind his tantrum, but that didn't stop me from walking over to T-Bone and placing my hand on his shoulder. My lips curled into a smirk as I told him, "If it means that much to you, you can call me hot stuff too."

"The hell he can," Caleb protested.

"You know what...*fuck it*. I don't give a rat's ass about any of it." He shook his head as he marched back over to the '57 Chevy he'd been working on. "Damn, I never learn."

When he started back to work, it was clear that he was done with his theatrics. I watched as Blaze went over to Clay and patted him on the shoulder. He whispered something in his ear, and Clay simply nodded and went back to taking out the trash. Caleb had also gone back to work, so I took that as my cue to head back to my paint room. I got busy stenciling the flame design on each of the front fenders, and it wasn't long before the workday came to an end. Knowing it wouldn't be long before Caleb was ready to go, I quickly removed my paint suit and rushed to the bathroom to try to fix myself up a bit. Even though today was about him seeing his parents for the first time since the day he'd left, I was nervous about meeting them. I was worried that my being there would only make things more difficult for him, but he didn't seem to care. He wanted me to be there with him, so I decided to suck it up and try to make the best of it.

I'd just finished touching up my makeup when Caleb tapped on the bathroom room. "You about ready to go?"

"Yep." I opened the door and smiled. "Ready as I'll ever be."

"Then, let's roll. I want to get there before dark."

I nodded and followed him out to the parking lot. When he got over to his Harley, he acted like it was nothing out of the norm as he threw his leg over the seat and waited for me to get on behind him. While we'd talked about it, I'd never actually ridden with him anywhere. We'd always ridden separately or taken my truck, so I was feeling a little skeptical as I slipped on my helmet and got on behind him. He started his engine, and after he put on his helmet, I placed my hands on his hips, bracing myself as he whipped out of the parking lot and onto the main road.

We hadn't been riding long when I suddenly realized why the other ol' ladies enjoyed riding with their men. While he was the one in control, riding in and out of traffic, I felt completely safe being there behind him. It was almost like we were one as we both leaned into a big curve, and I never once worried that he might put us in harm's way. I could just sit back and enjoy the ride, letting the wind whip around me as I took in the beautiful view, and I had no doubt that I would be riding with him again very soon. When we came up on a red light, he turned back to me and said, "You know, it feels good having you on the back of my bike."

"Yes, it does." Remembering the story of how he'd gotten his road name, I smiled as I teased, "Just be careful not to tip us over. I wouldn't want us to become a spot on the pavement."

"Hush, woman. You're safe with me."

Deciding not to torment him any further, I nodded. "Never doubted that for a minute."

As soon as the light changed, we were on our way again, and in no time, we were driving into Oakland. I knew we were getting closer to his folks' place and started to get nervous when we passed a few familiar hotspots of our old hometown. While I'd never been inside Caleb's house, I knew exactly where it was. I'd driven by the beautiful ranch-style house a million times when I was younger. It was nestled back in the middle of his father's cotton field with a driveway that seemed to go on for miles. I tried taking a deep breath to settle my nerves, but it was pointless. My heart started racing the second his house finally came into view. When he started down the long driveway, I felt Caleb's back stiffen, and I knew he was feeling just as nervous I was—if not more. I couldn't imagine what was going through his head as he parked next to the garage and got off his bike. It didn't help that he remained completely silent as he took off his helmet and waited for me to do the same.

My fingers trembled as I unlatched the chin strip and slipped it off my head. I quickly ran my fingers through my hair and smiled as I asked, "You ready?"

"Ready as I'll ever be."

He took my hand, and I followed as he started towards the front porch. We'd barely made it up the steps when the front door opened and his mother stepped outside. Her eyes widened in surprise as she stood there staring at Caleb in complete disbelief. After several long moments, tears started to fill her eyes as she muttered, "Caleb?"

"Hey, Mom." I could hear the strain in his voice as he continued, "I'm sorry to just show up unannounced like this, but I—"

Before he could finish his sentence, she rushed over and wrapped her arms around him as she cried, "I can't believe you're really here!"

He didn't speak. Instead, he just stood there holding her as she sobbed. He was still hugging her when his father suddenly appeared in the doorway. "Caleb?"

His mother quickly released her hold on Caleb and turned to her husband. "Can you believe it? He's really here."

Mr. Hughes didn't seem as pleased. In fact, he seemed downright disgusted as he stood there staring down at his son. He studied him for a moment, then turned and shook his head with repulsion when he spotted Caleb's Harley parked in the drive. He turned back to Caleb as he glared at his leather Satan's Fury cut. "So, you're what? A biker now? That's what you've chosen to do with your life?"

"Stan, please," Mrs. Hughes pleaded. "Don't."

"It's fine, Mom." Caleb looked up at his father as he told her, "I never expected him to understand."

"You're damn right, I don't understand!" He stepped

out onto the porch and motioned his hand out to the cotton fields behind him. "I spent my entire life busting my ass, morning, noon, and night, to provide for this family. I wanted you to have something you could be proud of. I wanted this land to be yours, and what did you do? You went and shit all over it!"

"I never wanted your land, Pop." I could see the emotion building behind his eyes as Caleb said, "Farming was never my thing. It was yours. I wanted something different."

"That's right. The big football star was too damn good to be a farmer." Anger flashed through his eyes as he glanced over at me. "Well, look at you now. A drug-addict biker who runs around with trash."

"You've crossed a line."

Ignoring Caleb's warning, his father grumbled, "A damn Harrington. Couldn't have gotten any lower if you tried."

Caleb took a charging step towards his father, but his mother placed her hand on his chest, stopping him. She scowled up at her husband as she shouted, "Stan! That's enough!"

"You're actually going to stand there and defend him after all he's done to this family!" He pointed his finger at Caleb as he snarled, "Don't forget that he's the one who hocked your mother's wedding ring, so he could buy—"

"I said, that's enough!"

"Fine. Have your little reunion." He turned and started back inside. "I'm done."

When the door slammed shut, Mrs. Hughes turned her attention back to Caleb. "I'm sorry, sweetheart. You know how your father can be. It'll just take him some time to come around."

"I know. It's fine. I just came here to let you both know

that I was okay." While he tried to play it off, I could tell he was hurting as he reached into his pocket and pulled out a slip of paper. He offered it to her as he said, "Here's my number. Just call if you ever need anything or just want to touch base."

"Okay." She reached out her hand as she turned to me and said, "I don't think we've had the pleasure. I'm Susan."

"Hi, Susan." I shook her hand. "I'm Darcy."

"It's such a pleasure to meet you." She smiled as she looked over to Caleb. "I take it you two are dating."

"We are." Caleb slipped his arm around my waist, pulling me closer. "She's the one who convinced me to come here today."

A soft smile crossed her face as she looked over to me and said, "I'll be forever grateful to you for that. I can't tell you how much it's meant to me to see that he's okay."

"You're very welcome."

We talked for a few more minutes, then Caleb announced, "It's getting late. We better get going."

"Okay." Susan reached out and hugged Caleb once more. "I'm really glad you came by. I hope you both will come again."

After we both said our goodbyes, neither of us spoke as we got back on his bike and started home. Caleb was quiet the entire way back to Memphis. I couldn't blame him, especially after the way his father had behaved. I'd had it in my mind that things would've gone better, but there was no way I could've known how his father would react. I just hoped that his mother was right, and that in time, his father would come around. I was still going over it all in my head when Caleb pulled up at my house. Still silent, we got off his bike and started inside. Once we were behind closed doors, I turned to him and said, "I'm really sorry about today. I had no idea it would play out like that."

"Nothing for you to be sorry about, Darcy. I knew what I was getting into when I went over there." He turned and placed his hands on his hips as he looked around my living room. "So, where do you want to start?"

Confused, I asked, "Start what?"

"Packing."

"Packing? What are you talking about?"

"Don't play dumb with me. It's beneath you." He slipped his arm around my waist as he pulled me over to him. "Now, answer the question. Where do you want to start packing?"

"So, we aren't even going to discuss what happened with your parents?"

"Nothing to talk about. Things played out exactly like I thought they would."

It was obvious that he didn't want to discuss it, but I just couldn't let it go. "I'm sorry that your father was—"

"An asshole?" he scoffed. "I'm used to it. I hate that he said what he did about you. I hope you know that it had nothing to do with you. It was all about him trying to get me where it hurts."

"Seemed he was pretty intent on making you feel bad. That's for sure."

"Like I said, things played out exactly like I thought they would. Eventually, he'll come around, and if he doesn't, then that's on him." His serious tone quickly changed as he said, "Now, enough about that. A deal's a deal. It's time to get this place packed up."

I wound my arms around his neck as I said, "So, we're really moving in together."

"We are, but that's just the beginning." He lowered his

mouth to my neck, kissing me lightly. "Once we get you settled, I'm gonna put a ring on your finger, and then—"

"Wait," I interrupted. "*A ring?*"

"You heard me." His eyes met mine in an intense gaze. "I want it all, Darcy, and I want it with you."

"Well, I guess that settles it. We're moving in together." As I looked around the room at all that needed to be packed, I told him, "We're going to need boxes. Lots and lots of boxes."

"We've got some over at the clubhouse. I'll call Clay and have him bring some over."

"Okay. I think there are some out back in the storage shed too."

After Caleb called Clay, we headed outside to the shed. As Caleb started gathering boxes, I found myself looking over at Maybell's place. I hadn't seen her since the day of KeShawn's funeral when I'd gone over to pay my respects. I was expecting her to be devastated by the loss of her grandson, but she seemed to be doing okay. In fact, she seemed to be doing better than okay. When I asked her about it, she simply said that she'd miss him, but she'd always known that it was only a matter of time before his bad decisions caught up with him. Maybell was a smart lady, smarter than I'd ever realized. I was still staring at her trailer when Caleb handed me a few boxes. "You okay?"

"Yep. I'm good."

I took the boxes from his hand and waited as he grabbed some more. We were on our way back inside, when I heard Ms. Frances ask, "Looks like you two have quite a project going on over there."

"Yes, ma'am. We do." With all the excitement, I'd forgotten about my two little guardian angels. They had been so good to me over the years, and it saddened me to think that I wouldn't be seeing them every morning and every afternoon. I was worried about their reaction as I told them, "I'm going to be moving in with Caleb."

"Oh, Darcy. That's wonderful news!" Mrs. Alice replied with unexpected excitement. "We're just so tickled for you."

"You are?"

"Of course, we are! We can both see that you've got yourself a good fella there. We knew it was only a matter of time before things would come to this," Mrs. Frances answered. "Now, don't get me wrong. We love having you here, and we're going to miss you terribly."

"I'm going to miss you too. Very much."

"Well, no one said you couldn't come visit now and then," Mrs. Alice teased. "In fact, we'll both be upset if you don't."

"I'll visit as often as I can."

"We know you will." Mrs. Frances turned her attention to Caleb as she said, "You better be good to our Darcy, or you'll have to answer to me. You got that?"

"Yes ma'am. I sure do," he replied with a smile. "But you don't have to worry. I have every intention of taking very good care of her."

"That's what I wanted to hear. Now, you two get in there and get to packing."

"Yes ma'am. We're on it."

As we started inside, Mrs. Alice called out to us, "If you need a break later, you're welcome to come over and have a toddy with us."

"Thanks. We might take you up on that."

Once we were inside, Caleb walked over to me and said, "I meant what I said out there. I'm going to do everything I can to make you happy."

"Don't you know?" I wound my arms around his neck. "You already have."

He leaned down and kissed me, long and hard, and as he held me in his arms, it hit me. Caleb Hughes was an essential part of my life. He was my past, my present, and now, he would be my future. He was mine, now and forever.

Epilogue

When I walked back into the bedroom, I found Darcy looking at herself in the mirror. She was wearing a pair of fitted jeans with a long-sleeve black top. Her long auburn hair was pulled back, revealing the delicate curves of her neck, and as usual, she looked incredible. I knew we were short on time, but I couldn't resist making my way over to her. As I came up behind her, I lowered my mouth to the nape of her neck and pulled her close as I trailed kisses down her shoulder. Staring at me through the mirror, Darcy warned, "*Caleb.*"

"Um-hmm."

I slipped my hands under the hem of her shirt as my hand drifted along her bare abdomen. She tilted her head back as she muttered, "We don't have time for this."

"For what?"

"To *mess around*," she fussed. "We need to go."

"We have a few minutes," I lied as I turned her to face me. Before she could argue, I pressed my mouth against hers with a kiss that was possessive and demanding, leaving no question as to what I had in mind for her. She gasped into my mouth when I pulled her hips to mine. "I need you...*now*."

"*Caleb*..." she breathed. As I'd hoped, her inhibitions fell away, and she reached up to remove my cut, quickly lowering it from my shoulders, then tossing it onto the bed. She bit her bottom lip as she lifted her arms over her head, waiting eagerly as I reached for the hem of her shirt and easing it over her head. So damn perfect.

My fingertips roamed over her bare skin, only stopping when I reached her breasts. I slipped my hands inside the cups of her bra, pulling them free. She couldn't stop herself from squirming as my hands traveled around her back to unhook her. Darcy's fingers gripped my shoulders as I lowered my head to her breast, flicking my tongue across her sensitive flesh. Her breath quickened as I moved to her other breast, and a shiver ran over her when the cold air hit the spot where my mouth had been.

I removed my mouth and hands from her breasts, letting her bra drift down, and then reached for her waist, unbuckling her jeans before I lowered them down her long legs to her ankles. I placed my hands on her bare hips and turned her around. She watched my reflection in the mirror as I trailed the tips of my fingers along her inner thigh, and her breath caught when I slipped my fingers between her legs. "I can't wait a second longer. I need to be inside you."

I quickly unfastened my belt and eased down my zipper, and she groaned with anticipation as I reached between us, positioning myself at her entrance. She placed her hands on the dresser bracing herself as I buried myself inside her with one hard thrust. "*Fuck!*"

A hiss escaped her lips as her body tightened around me. My hands reached up to cup her breasts as I started to rock forward with shallow thrusts. Her grip on the table tightened when I started driving into her with longer, deeper strokes. Her entire body trembled, and her breathing became ragged as her climax approached. She gasped with pleasure when I reached around and began teasing her with just enough pressure to send her over the edge.

"Oh, God! Don't stop," she cried while her orgasm surged through her body. My hands gripped her hips when her legs started to buckle and held her upright as she continued to spasm around me. My body tensed with my own impending release, and my thrusts became relentless as I quickened my pace. Seconds later, I came deep inside her with a satisfied growl echoing around the room. I didn't want to move. I just wanted to stay there until I was ready to go again, but then Darcy reminded me that I didn't have that luxury. "Umm, Caleb...We have to go."

"Just one more minute."

"We're going to be late."

"I don't care."

"Caleb," she fussed as she inched forward, breaking free from our embrace as she headed towards the bathroom. "We have to go."

I fastened my jeans, and as I pulled on my cut, I told her, "I'm ready when you are."

"Of course, you are," she said with a huff. "Why don't you just go start the truck. I'll be out in a minute."

"You got it."

I was on my way outside when my burner started ringing. I grabbed it out of my pocket, and when I looked down at the screen, I saw that it was my mother calling. Since the day I'd gone out to the house with Darcy, she'd been doing all she could to mend our broken relationship.

She called at least twice a week to check in, and even came out to the house to have dinner with Darcy and me. Unfortunately, Dad didn't come with her. He was still holding onto his grudge, but I hadn't given up hope on him—at least not yet. "Hey, Mom. How's it going?"

"It's going. You know how it is around here. Your father is still out in the fields, and I've been working on laundry. What about you?"

"Darcy and I were just about to walk out the door." As much as I hated to rush her, I didn't have a choice. "Was there something you needed?"

"Well, umm...Your father and I would like to invite you and Darcy over for dinner on Sunday. Nothing fancy. Just grilling burgers or something, and your sister and her new boyfriend will be here too."

"Dad knows about this?"

"Actually, it was his idea." She paused for a moment, then continued, "He wants to set things right, or at least try to."

"Kind of surprised to hear that."

"Your father is a stubborn man, but he loves you, Caleb. Give him a chance to fix this thing between you. If not for you, then do it for me, please?" she pleaded.

Hearing how much it meant to her, there was no way I could refuse. "We'll be there."

"Thank you, sweetheart. I'll see you both on Sunday."

I was just hanging up the phone when Darcy came out of the house. As she rushed towards the truck, she asked, "Who was that?"

"Mom," I answered as I got in and closed the door. As I started the engine, I told her, "I'll tell you about it on the way."

Just as I expected, Darcy was pleased to hear that my

father had finally started to come around. In fact, she was still going on about it when we arrived at the hospital. As we walked through the front doors, I couldn't help but think back to the last time we were all there. Kenadee was fighting for her life, and we were all worried that she and her baby might not survive. It was touch and go there for a while, especially at the beginning, but they both managed to pull through. We shouldn't have been surprised. Kenadee has always been tough, and we should've known that the same would hold true for their baby girl. When we walked into the waiting room, all of the guys were already there, talking amongst themseleves as they waited for news about the baby's delivery. Hoping that they wouldn't notice that we were the last to arrive, Darcy and I walked over and sat down with the others.

As soon as we were settled, Gunner leaned over to us and said, "I've seen that guilty look before."

"What guilty look?" Darcy asked feigning innocence.

"The guilty look you two were sporting when you came up in here late."

"We didn't have a guilty look," Darcy argued. "We were just a little frazzled from being caught up in traffic. That's all."

"Um-hmm. If you say so." Gunner smiled as he looked over to August and said, "See, I told you we wouldn't be the last ones here, and from the looks of it, they were up to the same thing we were."

August shook her head and sighed. "And now everybody knows why we were late, including my father."

All eyes darted over to Gus, and none of us were surprised to find him staring at Gunner with his eyebrow cocked and his arms crossed. Knowing there was nothing he could say in his defense, Gunner tried to divert the blame. "Not my fault. I was an innocent victim."

"Oh, please." August sighed. "Just stop while you're ahead."

Before he could bury himself any deeper, Blaze walked into the room with his daughter nestled in the crook of his arm. Kevin was standing proudly at his side as he announced, "Our Willow Grace is finally here!"

We all gathered around, congratulating him as we each took a peek at the newest addition to the family. As I stood there watching Blaze with his daughter, I couldn't help but smile. It was good to see him so happy. After all he'd been through, I didn't know a man on the planet who deserved it more. Knowing that Blaze and Willow needed to get back upstairs to Kenadee, the brothers and I said our goodbyes, and after promising to return soon, we each headed home. As Darcy and I walked out of the hospital, I thought back to the moment when Blaze first walked into the waiting room with Willow. Even though he was brag-ging that she twenty-one inches long and weighed eight pounds, six ounces, I couldn't get over how tiny she was. I glanced over at Darcy, and I couldn't help but wonder about the kids we'd have one day—a daughter with her thick auburn hair and a son with my crooked smile. I was lost in my thoughts when Darcy slipped her arm through mine and asked, "What are you smiling about over there?"

"Just thinking."

"About?" she pushed.

"Hmmm...About the house full of kids we're going to have one day."

"House full?" she gasped. "Seriously?"

"One, two...four or five." I reached for her and pulled her close. "I don't care."

"Okay. I can work with that." She wound her arms around my neck as she said, "Thank you."

"For?"

"Loving me the way you do." Emotion filled her eyes. "Until you, I'd never really known what it's like to truly be loved."

"Loving you is easy, Darcy."

"I don't know about that, but I do know you make me very happy."

"Well, get ready, baby, cause I'm just getting started."

THE END

Thanks so much for reading!
If you haven't had a chance to check out Gunner: Satan's Fury MC- Memphis, there is a short excerpt after the acknowledgments.

Be sure to sign up for my newsletter for updates on releases and chances to win giveaways. Here's the link:
http://eepurl.com/dvSpW5
Also-please follow me on BookBub: https://www.bookbub.com/authors/l-wilder

Acknowledgments

I am blessed to have so many wonderful people who are willing to give their time and effort to making my books the best they can be. Without them, I wouldn't be able to breathe life into my characters and share their stories with you. To the people I've listed below and so many others, I want to say thank you for taking this journey with me. Your support means the world to me, and I truly mean it when I say appreciate everything you do. I love you all!

PA: Natalie Weston

Editing/Proofing: Lisa Cullinan-editor, Rose Holub-Proofer, Honey Palomino-Proofer

Promoting: Amy Jones, Veronica Ines Garcia, Neringa Neringiukas, Whynter M. Raven

BETAS/Early Readers: Kaci Stewart, Tanya Skaggs, Jo Lynn, and Jessey Elliott

Street Team: All the wonderful members of Wilder's Women (You rock!)

Best Friend and biggest supporter: My mother (Love you to the moon and back.)

A short excerpt of Gunner: Satan's Fury MC-Memphis Book 5 is included in the following pages. Blaze, Shadow, Riggs, Murphy and Gus are also included in this Memphis series, and you can find them all on Amazon. They are all free with KU.

EXCERPT FROM GUNNER: SATAN'S FURY MC- MEMPHIS

Her Goodbye

August 19, 1994

Gus,

I've been lying here watching you sleep for hours, just thinking about the time we've shared together. This summer has been the best few months of my life. I can honestly say I've never been happier, and that's all because of you. I love you, Gus. I love you with every fiber of my being. You mean so much to me, more than I thought possible. With you, I've learned how it feels to truly love and to be loved. That's why this letter is so hard to write.

I've done a lot of thinking over the past few weeks, and I've come to realize that it doesn't matter how much I love you or you love me. It just isn't enough. We're from two different worlds, headed down two completely different paths, and if we stay together, we're only going to end up destroying one another. I can't bear for that to happen. I love you too much. It breaks my heart to say this to you, but I'm leaving Memphis. I am asking you to please respect my decision. Don't try to find me. Don't call me. Let me find a way to move on, and I will do the same for you. It's the only way either of us will ever make it through this.

This wasn't an easy decision for me. In fact, it's killing me to walk away from you, but deep down I know it's the right thing to do. Please remember—I love you today, I loved you yesterday, and I will love you tomorrow and always. That will never change.

Love,
   Samantha

Prologue

When I joined the Marines, I didn't have any preconceived notions about being in the military and going to war. I'd seen and heard enough to know it wasn't going to be easy—far from it. It was one of the hardest, but greatest, things I'd ever done. I worked my ass off, fought for my country, and learned just how far I could be pushed without breaking. But it came at a price. Every waking moment I'd wondered if my time was about to run out, if I'd seen my last sunset or had lain my head down on my pack for the very last time. Even if I'd managed to survive long enough to see the sunrise the next morning, there'd been little consolation in knowing I'd just have to go through that same hell all over again.

I thought I'd find peace once I was finally back in the States with my family and friends and able to sleep in my own bed or walk down the street without feeling like I was under a constant threat—but I'd been wrong. I never realized just how wrong until a shotgun wound forced me to go home.

WHEN I GOT OFF THE PLANE, I FOUND MY MOTHER waiting for me at the gate. As expected, she was alone and still wearing her green Food and More grocery smock. Her tired eyes filled with tears the second she spotted me walking in her direction. "Cade!" she called, rushing towards me with her arms opened wide.

She was just about to reach for me when she suddenly stopped and looked down at my arm. After getting shot in the shoulder, I had to have reconstructive surgery, which meant wearing a sling for the next couple of months. "I'm okay, Mom."

She eased up on her tiptoes and carefully wrapped her arms around my neck, giving me one of her famous mom hugs. Damn. I was a grown man, and her hugs still got to me the same way they did when I was a kid. "I can't tell you how good it is to see you, sweetheart."

"Good to see you too."

"I've been worried sick about you. Your father has too."

"I know." I gave her a quick squeeze, then said, "I'm sorry I worried you."

"I'm just glad you're home where we can take care of you." She gave me a little pat as she stepped back and smiled. "Have to fatten you up a bit."

I was six-four and weighed about two hundred and forty pounds. Before I was shot, I worked out every day and knew what condition I was in. I glanced down at myself and told her, "I'm not exactly skin and bones here, Mom."

"Well, you look like you've lost weight to me ... and you're a little peeked."

"Yeah, well ... you'd look a little peeked too if you'd just spent the last sixteen hours on an airplane." Before she could respond, I added, "Let me grab my bag, and then we can get out of here."

As she followed me over to the baggage claim area, she explained, "Your father wanted to come tonight, but you know how he is around crowds. We both figured it would be easier if he just waited at the house for us."

My father was a brilliant man. There wasn't a mathematical problem he couldn't figure out, which made him one of the best accountants in town. But he'd always been a little *different*. He wasn't a fan of crowds or loud noises. He'd fixate on things from historical facts to the changes in weather, obsessing on every detail, and he wasn't exactly big on showing affection—except for when he was with my mother. He'd always been different with her—touching her, holding her hand, and even hugging her. I'd always hoped that some of that would rub off on me, but it never did. "It's fine, Mom. I wasn't expecting him to be here."

"Well, he's really looking forward to seeing you."

Even though I knew that wasn't true, I replied, "I'm looking forward to seeing him too."

"Oh, and Brooklyn should be home by the time we get there."

As I lifted my duffle-bag off the conveyer belt, I asked, "She been making it okay?"

"You know your sister ... she's always on the go." Mom shrugged. "But I guess that's a good thing. It keeps her out of trouble."

We headed outside to the parking garage, and once we got to Mom's car, she popped the trunk and I tossed my bag inside. I slammed it shut and then we both got in the car and started home. We hadn't been driving long when I heard her let out a deep sigh. I glanced over at her, and even in the dark, I could see the dark circles under her eyes. "Have you been working double shifts again?"

"No ... it's just been a long week."

"Why's that?"

"Let's not talk about that right now," she interrupted, then quickly changed the subject. "I've got your room all ready for you and got your rehab appointments all lined up. CJ and Dalton are planning to come by and see you once you get settled."

"That'd be cool."

It had been years since I'd seen my best friends from high school. We'd all gone our separate ways, so I was surprised when she said, "Did you know that CJ and his girlfriend, Adeline, are expecting?"

"Hadn't heard that."

"I don't think it was something they were planning, but ... you know how those things go."

Mom continued to ramble on about all the latest gossip in town until we pulled up in the driveway. As soon as she'd parked, I got out, grabbed my bag, and followed her up to the front door. She motioned for me to go inside as she said, "You get settled, and I'll go start dinner. I'm making pork chops and mashed potatoes."

"Okay, sounds good." When I walked into the living room, I found Dad sitting in his recliner with his TV tray in front of him. He was studying one of his patches through a magnifying glass, something I'd seen him do a thousand times before. It was a hobby that started when he was a kid. In hopes of helping him make friends, his folks had signed him up for the Boy Scouts. While their plan for him to make friends didn't pan out, he did gain an interest in patches. That interest turned into an obsession

—an obsession that carried over into his adulthood. He didn't even look up when I walked over to him. "Hey, Pop. How's it going?"

"Good."

I swallowed back the feeling of rejection that was creeping up inside of me and tried once again to get his attention. "You get some new patches?"

"Um-hmm." Without turning to look at me, he held up the long, narrow patch and said, "It's an Unteroffizier-vorschule cuff title."

"I got no idea what that is, Pop."

Like he was reading straight from the encyclopedia, he spouted off, "*Unteroffiziervorschule* is German for NCO Preparatory School. The German military created the school to train lower ranks in leadership and initiative. Their students eventually became commissioned officers."

"Wow, that's really something."

"Also found a set of World War II German rural police collar tabs.

"Oh, really?" There was a time when it bothered me that my father showed me little to no attention, but as I grew older, I realized that it wasn't his fault. My father had Asperger's Syndrome. I had no choice but to accept the fact that he'd never be the kind of father I hoped he would be. "Are those good ones?"

Like a child, he brought it close to his body, protecting it as he answered, "Yes. Very good."

"That's great, Pop." As I started towards my room, I told him, "I'm gonna go get settled in." Without replying, he turned his attention back to his magnifying glass, and just like always, it was like I'd never been in the room.

I went upstairs to my room and lay across the bed. As I stared up at my old Bon Jovi poster, I was surprised by how different it felt to be here. Everything was exactly the way I'd left it, but for some reason, everything in the whole fucking house seemed different. What had once felt like home was now completely foreign to me.

Over the next few days that feeling had only grown stronger. When my buddies from high school had come by to see me, it was like they were complete strangers. After the first few minutes, the conversations became forced and awkward. I couldn't even talk to my mother and sister. It was like I was stuck inside my head and couldn't find the right words to say to anyone. I'd told myself it would pass, that things would get back to normal eventually, but they didn't. With each new day, things only seemed to get be getting worse. Hell, even the shit with my father was fucking with my head. He'd never talked to me or showed that he gave a damn about me, and I'd adapted to that. I'd stopped hoping that things would change, but I could feel the resentment building inside of me, making me feel like I was going to explode at any minute. I just couldn't take it. I needed to get the fuck out of that house and out of my head, or I was going to lose my mind. I grabbed my keys and headed downstairs. Just as I was about to walk out the front door, Mom called out to me, "Cade? Wait! Where are you going?"

"I'm going out."

"Again?" Confusion crossed her face. "Is something wrong?"

"No, Mom. I'm just—"

She gave me one of her looks as she interrupted, "You're just *what*, Cade?"

"I can't do this anymore. It's just too much."

"What are you talking about? What's too much?"

"*Everything*. This house. This town." I let out an aggravated breath as I grumbled, "*Dad*."

"I know it's not easy coming home after all you've been through, but we love you, sweetheart. We like having you here with us."

"Why do you keep saying *we*?" I huffed. "Dad could care less if I'm alive or dead."

"That's not true, Cade. Your father loves you."

I shook my head as I argued, "Yeah, right. He's never once given me a second thought, and you damn well know it."

"Come with me. I want to show you something." She walked into my dad's office and over to the glass case where he kept his prized patches. As she opened the top latch, she explained, "A few days after you left for training, your father started a new collection."

I glanced down at the case and my chest tightened as soon as I saw it was lined with various Marine Corp patches, from the seal and crest to old veteran patches. "There's so many of them."

"I know, honey. He might not be good at showing it, but you've been on his mind every day."

I could feel the emotion building inside of me as I muttered, "I didn't know."

"I know." Mom had always understood my father in a way I never could. As far as I could tell, my father had never given me a second thought, but as she stood there staring down at those patches, she seemed to think otherwise. She slipped her arm around my back, doing her best to reassure me as she said, "That's why I wanted you to see this."

It meant a lot to me to see those patches, to know that I'd crossed my father's mind. That realization made me feel like the walls were closing in on me. I couldn't breathe. I needed to get some air before I totally lost it. I leaned over and kissed her cheek. "I'll be back in a couple of hours."

I rushed out of the house, got in my truck, and cranked the engine. There was only one place for me to escape the thoughts that were rushing through my head—Danver's Pub. When I walked in, it looked exactly how it did five years ago. They were even playing the same damn songs on the jukebox, but I didn't give a rat's ass about the music or the décor. I needed a fucking drink. Hell, I needed a slew of them. I went over to the counter, placed my order for three shots of chilled vodka, and downed them one right after the other. I ordered three more, immediately knocking them down, and was about to order three more when a man came over and sat down next to me. I took a quick glance at him and an uneasy feeling washed over me when I saw that he was wearing a Satan's Fury cut. Their MC was known for being a group of badasses who didn't take shit from anyone, and from the looks of the patch he was sporting, this guy next to me was the biggest badass of them all. He was a big guy, maybe in his late forties, but he was fit and looked like he could hold his own and then some. He called the bartender over and said, "Bring us another round."

The bartender nodded, then placed six shot glasses on the counter, quickly filling them to the brim. "Anything else?"

"For now ... just keep my tab running." He lifted one of the shot glasses and asked, "You got a name, kid?"

"Cade."

"Couldn't help but notice the military cut. You in the service?"

"I was." I ran my hand over the top of my head as I replied, "I just got back a few days ago."

"Well, here's to you, Cade. Thanks for your service." He motioned his hand towards my round of shots and waited for me to lift mine, and then we both threw them back. "So, you got plans to go back?"

"Nah. Pretty sure that chapter of my life has closed. My shoulder guaranteed that."

"What's up with your shoulder?"

"Bullet fucked up my rotator cuff."

"Damn." He shook his head as he reached for a another shot. "That's a tough one, but you're young, you'll be back like new before you know it."

"You sound pretty sure of yourself."

"That's because I am," he said, then he pulled back the sleeve of his t-shirt, revealing a wound similar to mine. "Hurt like a bitch, but eventually healed and so will yours."

"Good to know." I took another shot, then immediately reached for the next. "Thanks for the round."

"Least I can do. After all, you seem pretty damn determined to get tanked tonight, so I thought I'd help you out."

"Needed to clear my head."

"Vodka isn't gonna help you with that."

"Maybe not, but after the day I've had, it's worth a try."

"Been one of those days, huh?"

"Yeah," I muttered. "You could say that."

"Life has a way of throwing some pretty hard punches … some harder than others." He looked me dead in the eye. "You've just gotta take the hit and find a way to get back up."

"I've had one too many hits, man. Not sure I see the point in getting back up anymore."

"Put your hand on your heart." He waited silently as I did as he requested. "You feel that? As long as your heart's beating, then you've got a purpose. You've just gotta figure out what it is."

"I'm trying, but it's just so damn hard." I ran my hand down my face and sighed. "Every fucking thing is exactly the same as it was when I left ... my folks, my house, this whole damn city, but it feels so different. How is that possible?"

"Because you've changed. You can't expect things to be the same when you're not the same man you were when you left."

"I'm still me, though."

"Yeah, but now you're a different version of yourself." His eyes narrowed as he asked, "You ever ridden before?"

"A motorcycle?"

"Not talking about a fucking moped, son," he scoffed.

I shrugged. "Ridden a couple of times when I was younger but never actually had one of my own."

"Might be time to try again."

"Maybe so."

"*Maybe* isn't an answer, son." Then he leaned towards me and said, "If I've learned anything in this life, it's that we only regret the chances we didn't take. It's time for you to take that chance."

"I hear ya." I reached for my last shot and added, "But I don't own a motorcycle, and even if I did, I couldn't ride with this shoulder."

"That's two problems, son." He chuckled. "Both can be solved with time."

He reached into his pocket, pulled out a card, and offered it to me. "The name's Gus. When you get back on your feet, come by the clubhouse. We'll take that ride together."

"Sounds good. I'll do that."

"I'll be looking forward to it." After finishing off his last shot, he stood up and started to walk away. "Drink to your heart's content. Just be sure to get a ride home, son."

"Will do."

There was something about the way he'd called me *son* that got to me. As odd as it seemed, it felt like he actually meant it. Until that moment, I hadn't realized how much I needed to hear it. That one word had me looking down at the card Gus had given me, and I knew at that moment I would be taking that ride with him. What I didn't know was how that decision would change my life forever.

Gunner

"Give me a second," I called out to Blaze. "I'll be right back."

"Whoa ... Where are you going?" His eyes narrowed as he watched me start across the parking lot. "We're going to be late."

I was following Blaze, Shadow, Murphy, and their ol' ladies into the gas station when a gorgeous brunette in the parking lot caught my attention. She was pacing back and forth in front of her car. I couldn't tell for sure, but it looked like she was crying as she talked to someone on her cell phone. When we came back out and she was still there, I figured something must be wrong. There was something about a woman in need that got to me, especially when she was smoking hot with curves made for sin. As I continued walking towards her, I glanced back at Blaze and said, "No, we won't. I'll just be a minute."

"Um-hmm. I've heard that shit before," he complained. Murphy, the club's sergeant-at-arms, was a good guy, always played by the rules and never let a brother down, so I wasn't surprised when he said, "We still gotta drop the girls off, and if we're late for church, Gus is gonna be pissed."

"I already told ya ... We won't be late."

As I made my way closer to the woman, I heard her say, "Are you sure about this?" A gust of wind whipped passed us, and I quickly became mesmerized by the way her long, dark hair fluttered around her face. Damn. It was like I'd been pulled into some romantic, chick flick where everything was moving in slow motion. I needed to shake it off before I made a fucking fool of myself. She tucked her hair behind her ears as she continued, "I'm not certain. I think I'm close, but I took the wrong exit. Don't worry, I'll figure it out." After another brief pause, she said, "I'll let you know."

When she ended the call, I put on my best smile and asked, "You lost, darlin'?"

The gorgeous brunette glanced up at me for a moment, and her dark eyes quickly drifted over me. Clearly unaffected by my dashing good looks, she looked down at her phone and replied, "No."

"You sure about that ... 'cause you're a long way from heaven."

I cocked my head to the side and smiled, hoping she'd find the humor in my corny pickup line. Sadly, she was totally unfazed. Instead, my words just hung in the air, completely disregarded as she stared down at her phone. "I'm sure you're a nice enough guy and all, but I really don't have time for this right now."

"Okay, then. Tell me how I can help." I wasn't sure what to make of her. I knew she wasn't from around here, otherwise she'd know how dangerous it was for her to be standing out in the parking lot with every thug around checking her out. I couldn't blame them. Hell, she looked like a knockout in those hip-hugging jeans and low-cut t-shirt. I could only imagine what she'd look like wearing nothing at all. Just the thought made it difficult not to readjust myself. Unfortunately, I didn't have the same effect on her. In fact, she seemed unimpressed by my southern charm and was doing her best to disregard me completely. I could've just walked away, kept what was left of my ego intact, but that would have been too easy. "Seriously ... you got any idea where you are?"

"Actually, I do. I'm in Memphis and"—she glanced up at the store front sign— "at the Citgo gas station on Frayser Road."

"So, you know you're in Frayser?"

"Umm ... Yeah." Her eyebrows furrowed as she asked, "Why?"

"Not exactly safe around here, darlin'." I lifted my chin, motioning my head towards the hood-rats smoking dope at the side of the building. "There are some real bad folks around these parts."

Her gazed drifted downward as she took a moment to study my torn jeans, leather cut, and tattoos. She shook her head, then clipped, "And what about you? Are you one of them?"

"Depends on who you ask."

"Um-hmm. If had to guess, I would say you and your friends are just as dangerous, *if not more so*, as those men over there." With a cocked brow and a half-smile, she sassed, "Regardless, I'd already be gone if you weren't here ... *you know*, distracting me."

"Well, that's as much your fault as it is mine." I let my eyes slowly drift over her, taking my time to study every gorgeous inch of her, as I said, "If you weren't so damn beautiful, I wouldn't be over here talking to you. Besides, I had to at least try and see if there was something I could do to help. Wouldn't want anything to happen to you while you were out here all alone."

"You're good. I'll give you that." She shook her head and scoffed, "A regular knight in shining armor, but you're wasting your time with me. I'm fine."

"I don't know about that." A smirk crossed my face as I added, "This is no place for someone like you, so if you're lost, I'll be glad to help you find wherever it is you're trying to go."

"Thanks, but I think I've got it figured out." She got in her car, and just before she closed her door, she looked over to me and said, "Maybe you'll have better luck with your next damsel in distress."

Before I had a chance to respond, she started her car and drove out of the parking lot. I watched as she pulled out onto the main road, and moments later, her tail lights disappeared into the traffic. When I turned around, I found the guys sitting on their Harleys with their ol' ladies, watching me with goofy grins plastered across their faces. Doing my best to ignore them, I walked over, got on my bike, and started up my engine, revving it several times. My brothers never moved. They just sat there staring at me like three jackasses. "What?"

"Is your bike burning oil?" Blaze poked with a shit-eating grin on his face. "Oh, no. That's just *you*."

"What are you talking about?"

"Your ass just got smoked."

"What the fuck are you talking about? I didn't get smoked."

Shaking his head, Shadow asked, "You get her number ... or even her fucking name?"

"No."

Shadow was the club's enforcer. He was usually pretty quiet, keeping to himself and remaining eerily intense. He wasn't normally one to fuck around, but that didn't keep him from joining in. "Then, *your ass just got smoked*."

"Fuck y'all."

Rider shrugged. "We're just calling 'em like we see 'em."

"Well, you saw this one wrong. I wasn't trying to pick that chick up," I argued. "I was being a Good Samaritan."

"Um-hmm ... You know, we aren't buying that shit for one minute, brother," Shadow taunted. "Just admit it. You've lost your edge. Hell, it's gotten so bad you can't even pick up a chick in the fucking hood."

"Give the guy a break," Alex fussed. She was Shadow's ol' lady and a real sweetheart of a chick. I'd always thought a lot of her, especially now. "At least he tried."

"Tried and failed," Blaze joked.

Kenadee leaned forward as she looked over to me and said, "Don't let them get to you, Gunner. You can't win them all."

"Thanks, Kenadee." Before the guys had a chance to respond, I started to back out and said, "I thought we had to get to the girls home."

Blaze looked over to Shadow and Murphy as he said, "He's right. We better get going."

With a quick nod, they each started up their engines, and one by one, we backed out of the gas station. As we pulled out of the lot, I thought back to the beautiful brunette and cursed myself for not trying harder to get her number. I could tell just by looking at her that she was one of those once-in-a-lifetime kind of women. I hated that I'd let her slip through my fingers, but in truth, I knew it was all for the best. I didn't need the distraction, especially with a run coming up. Since the day Gus became president of the Memphis chapter, he'd worked his ass off to make it what it is today—one of the most notorious clubs in the South. It hadn't been easy. Shit, it took one hell of a fight to take claim to such a dangerous territory, but he'd done it. More than that, he'd managed to do it without compromising his beliefs. He always remained loyal to his brothers, always putting us above all else—even if that meant putting his needs second. It was no wonder that we all respected him and followed him without question.

I tagged along as Murphy and the others dropped their ol' ladies off, then followed them over to the clubhouse. By the time we arrived, the others had already started to gather in the conference room. Gus had called us all in to go over the final details of the run, ensuring that we all knew exactly what was expected before, during, and afterward. This particular run meant a great deal to us all. Gus had worked with Cotton, the president of the Washington chapter, to create a pipeline among several of the other chapters, enabling us to distribute twice the product in half the time. Since its creation, our shipments had almost doubled in size, making this one of our biggest deliveries to date. It was important for us to make sure that everything went exactly as planned.

Once everyone was seated, Gus stood up and said, "I want to make something clear with you boys. I know this isn't the first time we've done this particular run. By now, you should be feeling pretty comfortable with the way things are run, but I don't want you letting that get in your head. This is no time for any of you to be getting comfortable. You gotta keep your head in the fucking game. Stay alert. Be looking for problems before they arise. Watch your back. Always assume that someone's watching, 'cause if we don't stay vigilant with this thing, we're gonna lose everything we've worked for. You got me?"

"Understood. We won't let you down, Prez," Riggs assured him.

"I know you won't, son. None of you will." His expression softened as he added, "We all had different reasons for joining Fury. The way of life. The freedom. The ride. Whatever brought us here, we all stayed for the same reason ... Family. There's not a one of us in this club who wouldn't take a bullet for the other, and that alone is what keeps us going. Even when shit gets hard ... so hard you think it'll break ya, you always know you've got a brother who has your back. So, remember that as you get ready for this run. I want every one of you doing your part to make sure this goes off without a hitch."

FOR MORE, BE SURE TO CHECK OUT GUNNER: SATAN'S Fury MC-Memphis on Amazon.

Made in the USA
Coppell, TX
22 January 2020